Elle shook her head violently. "There's no way I'm not going to be involved in this. But let me get Daisy ready. She knows Lily's scent." She patted the dog's head.

He smiled. She was right. This dog was probably their best bet in tracking down the women. "Go for it. I'll meet you around back." Her jaw was set, and where there had once been fear in her eyes, the look was now replaced with rage. He could understand it. "Again, Elle, if you change your mind about going along, all you have to do is let me know—we can get another handler in here. Sometimes when we're too close to a case, it can take a lot out of us."

"It's far harder on me knowing that Lily and Catherine are out there somewhere, possibly hurt, and I'm doing nothing about it. There's not a chance in hell I'm going to change my mind."

ACKNOWLEDGMENTS

This book would not have been possible without a great team of people, including my editors who had to patiently wait on my broken butt. Don't worry, I'm fine now—just very appreciative for kind people in a world where chaos is the order of the day.

I'd also like to extend special thanks to Detective Sergeant Ryan Prather of the Missoula Sheriff's Department, who walked me through handgun training and building clearing; the K-9 unit from the Gallatin County Sheriff's Department, who showed me exactly how amazing well-trained K-9s are; and last to the cutest EOD rottweiler on the planet— Daisy—and her kind handler, Troy Kechely.

A great deal of research has gone into this and every book I write, so any errors are solely my fault, and I apologize in advance for any perceived mistakes. This author is far from perfect but loves to create stories that will always keep you, my readers, turning the page.

Thank you for reading.

K-9 RECOVERY

———

DANICA WINTERS

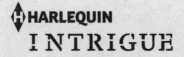

HARLEQUIN
INTRIGUE

To the men and women in blue who serve our great nation. Thank you and your families for your sacrifices.

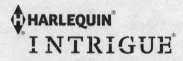

Recycling programs for this product may not exist in your area.

ISBN-13: 978-1-335-55529-8

K-9 Recovery

Copyright © 2021 by Danica Winters

This edition published by arrangement with Harlequin Books S.A.

For questions and comments about the quality of this book, please contact us at CustomerService@Harlequin.com.

Harlequin Enterprises ULC
22 Adelaide St. West, 40th Floor
Toronto, Ontario M5H 4E3, Canada
www.Harlequin.com

Printed in U.S.A.

Danica Winters is a multiple-award-winning, bestselling author who writes books that grip readers with their ability to drive emotion through suspense and occasionally a touch of magic. When she's not working, she can be found in the wilds of Montana, testing her patience while she tries to hone her skills at various crafts—quilting, pottery and painting are not her areas of expertise. She believes the cup is neither half-full nor half-empty, but it better be filled with wine. Visit her website at danicawinters.net.

Books by Danica Winters

Harlequin Intrigue

STEALTH: Shadow Team

A Loaded Question
Rescue Mission: Secret Child
A Judge's Secrets
K-9 Recovery

Stealth

Hidden Truth
In His Sights
Her Assassin For Hire
Protective Operation

Mystery Christmas

Ms. Calculation
Mr. Serious
Mr. Taken
Ms. Demeanor

Smoke and Ashes
Dust Up with the Detective
Wild Montana

Visit the Author Profile page at Harlequin.com.

CAST OF CHARACTERS

Elle Spade—A K-9 trainer working with the cutest dog on the planet, Daisy. When she is called in on a special assignment to help with a little girl, all of her skills as a trainer and as a member of STEALTH: Shadow Team come into question.

Sergeant Grant Anders—A man as sexy as his name and as deadly with a gun as he is devilish with his stare. Known for his stoicism and old-school ways, he's the last man Elle wants to have to work with, and yet she is forced to join the task force in order to do their jobs.

Zoey Martin—The team leader for the STEALTH organization and head honcho of the Shadow Team.

Senator Dean Clark—Lily Clark's father and a man who may or may not be the exact stereotypical politician. Only time will tell if he can be trusted or if he is one of their lead suspects.

Catherine Clark—Lily Clark's mother, but first and foremost a fan of high society and keeping an image that is more pristine than her white designer handbag.

Lily Clark—A three-year-old little girl with a heart of gold and two absentee parents. All she wants is someone to love her, and that someone is the last person anyone thought...the battle-scarred Elle Spade.

Steve Rubbic and Philip Crenshaw—Two men who have individually emailed credible death threats to the senator about killing and maiming his family... and both mean business.

Chapter One

Love was a language everyone spoke, but few were fluent. Elle was definitely one of those who struggled.

It wasn't the concept of love that she found difficult to embrace—a union of souls so enmeshed that nothing and no one could come between them. At least, that was what the fairy tales that had been spoon-fed to her as a child and adolescent had told her. Perhaps it was these insipid stories that had set her up for failure in the relationship department. According to those stories, love was built on a foundation of ball gowns, champagne and whispers of forever, while reality peppered her with missed dates, drunken late-night phone calls and broken promises. As far as she could tell, love was all a lie.

The three-year-old girl standing before her was just another reminder of the consequences to the innocent when lies and love went too far.

"Ms. Elle?" she said, her voice high and pleading, though she had asked no real question.

"What is it, Lily babe?" Elle smiled down at the little blonde whose hands were covered with the remnants of cotton candy and pocket lint. She reached into her purse and pulled out a packet of baby wipes.

She was really starting to get this whole caretaker thing down.

"No," Lily said, pouting as she put her hands behind her back and stuffed her cherubic cheeks into the shoulder of her jacket.

Or maybe Elle wasn't doing quite as well as she thought.

"Just a quick wipe and then you can head back out to the swings. Okay?"

"I want juice." Lily smiled, her eyes big and bright. It reminded Elle of her dog, Daisy.

She put the wipes back and handed her a box of apple juice from her bag. "Only one, okay?"

Lily didn't say anything as she took the juice box, walked over to the sandbox and plopped down, already chatting with a new friend.

She had just been worked over by a toddler. *Damn.*

Before long, and after a series of carefully constructed arguments on Lily's side, they found themselves headed back to the Clark house. They walked up the steps to the front door of the colonial-style home, a throwback to the type of residence built by people who'd come to the wilderness of Montana to make their fortunes—and succeeded. The house was hardly the only sign of generational wealth. Everything, down to the three-year-old's shoes, wing tips she would likely only wear once, spoke of what old money could buy.

When Elle had been three, she had been running barefoot through the sands of Liberia while her parents were taking contracts and acting as spooks for the United States government. Though they had been gone for several years now, she missed them.

The door swung open before they even reached it, and Catherine stepped out. She sent Elle a composed smile, the woman's trademark—a look of benevolence and influence all wrapped into one.

"She was perfect, as per usual," Elle said, watching as Lily slipped behind her mother's legs and disappeared into the belly of the house without so much as a backward wave. "Bye, little one!" she called after Lily.

It was a good thing she wasn't a sensitive soul or the little girl's apathy at her leaving would have broken her heart. Actually, it did hurt a little, but she would never let it show.

Catherine looked after her daughter but didn't say anything as the girl shuffled up the stairs.

Watching Lily's toddling steps up made Elle's skin prickle. She couldn't believe Catherine was letting the girl ascend to the second floor without a helping hand. One little slip, one poorly planted foot and Lily could have been lost to them all—and that girl was a gift. Everywhere she went she left the glitter of laughter.

"Do you want me to help her up to her room?" Elle said, stepping into the parlor.

"No," Catherine said, waving her off.

In the living room to her left, there was a group of men standing around and talking. They were all wearing suits and ties, except one, who was dressed in khakis and had a stinking cigar wedged into the corner of his mouth and a tumbler of scotch in his hand. The men looked like models for a fraternity's alum party or a political gathering.

"Thank you for taking her. It is appreciated." Catherine reached over for her purse, like she was going to pay Elle as if she was nothing more than a teenage babysitter.

She stopped her with a wave of her hand. "No, ma'am, please don't."

"I know I pay your company, but you need a tip at the very least."

She wasn't an hourly charge kind of woman,

and the only reason she had agreed to take this security position was because she was the most temperate of the Spades. The boys would have handled the little girl like she was an egg, especially given the fact that Lily's father was a senator.

Elle couldn't give two shakes who the girl's parents were, except right now, when she was forced to face the fact that Catherine's focus was on her friends and not on her baby. Elle hadn't even seen the senator since she had taken the security position three months ago.

She had to reserve her judgments about the family. Her interactions were limited to drop-offs, pickups and little else. Catherine had made a point of not letting her interact with Lily when she was around.

Catherine stuffed a $100 bill into her hand. Part of her wanted to throw it on the ground and tell her to screw off, but instead she slipped it into her pocket. As she did, Catherine closed the door in her face.

It was no wonder the woman's daughter wasn't the kind for long goodbyes.

Maybe she didn't have to reserve judgments after all—Catherine was a brat.

That would make it easier to say goodbye when this security detail came to an end. But it was going to be tough to say goodbye to Lily.

As she walked to her truck, she took one long look back at the house. Lily was sitting in her bedroom window looking out. When she spotted her, the little girl waved.

Yes, saying goodbye would be hard.

As she got into her truck, she sighed and then rolled out toward the ranch. The miles drifted by as she forced herself to think about something other than the little girl. Tonight, she was supposed to have Daisy work with members of the local sheriff's department, who had graciously offered up their Search and Rescue and training warehouse as well as give assistance in running hides.

Daisy had come so far in just a couple of years; from a crazy little rottweiler puppy, she had turned into a dog that was capable of finding a castaway shoe in a rainstorm from a half mile away. She wasn't perfect—there would always be off days—but she was better than even Elle could have hoped.

When she made it home to the Widow Maker Ranch, Daisy was waiting for her at her little cabin. Her nubby black tail whipped back and forth violently as Elle walked in. The dog spun in excited circles, prancing, her face as close to a human smile as it could get.

Yes, she loved that dog. So had Lily, until her

mother had put a stop to her bringing Daisy onto the property—even when only in her vehicle.

Loading Daisy and the gear up into the truck, she made her way over to the training warehouse. They hadn't worked there before; mostly she had worked with the K-9 units from the city police department, so this would be a fun, new experience.

Arriving, she found a tall, brooding sheriff's officer standing beside the bay doors. He was doing something on his phone, and he looked put out that he was standing in the icy near dark of the late winter night. Most people she worked with forgot any apprehensions the moment they saw Daisy. She was beautiful, with her gleaming black coat and buckskin-colored face and paws, and a blaze mark on her chest. And she loved everyone.

The man looked up from his phone, and his eyes flashed bright green in the thin light. He was stocky, and he wore a knit cap. When he gazed at her, he smiled for a split second, but as quickly as the sexy smile came, it disappeared and was replaced with what she assumed was a trademark scowl.

"You were supposed to be here ten minutes ago." He stuffed his phone away.

She wasn't late, she was never late, and the accusation made her hackles raise. She wanted to growl back at him and tell him to look at his watch, but she resisted the urge. They were here at the sheriff's invitation. Clearly this man wasn't here of his own volition.

"There must have been a miscommunication. Sorry about that." She was careful not to put the apology on herself or her mistake. If anything, he should be apologizing for the lack of a professional and warm welcome.

He said something under his breath.

It was a good thing he was handsome and she wanted this hour to train with Daisy, or she would have told him to pound sand then and there. She hated not having the upper hand. If he was sexist, too…she would be out of here in no time. Daisy could train somewhere else.

"If you like, I can come back another time." When someone else wanted to work with her and Daisy.

He sighed, the sound resigned. "We're both here."

She flipped her keys in her hand, thinking about how easy it would be to get in her truck and start the engine.

"Look," she said, her frustration finally threatening to come to a full boil, "if you don't want to do this, it's okay. I can promise you that I'm trustworthy and Daisy and I can use the training warehouse without supervision. You can just unlock the door and go. I will lock up when we're done. No big deal," she said, giving him the out he appeared to want.

His whole body shifted, like he suddenly must have realized how he was coming off to her. "No, no. As one of the search and rescue coordinators, I'm more than happy to help." He turned to the door and entered the code. The garage door ground open, exposing the interior of the building.

One side of the warehouse kept a variety of trucks, rafts, snowmobiles and mobile command units marked with the Missoula County Search and Rescue badge. The other half of the warehouse had been set up to look like a makeshift house.

She led Daisy out of the back seat of the truck and clicked her onto her lead. He had his back turned to them and didn't seem to notice the dog.

It was silly, but Elle was a bit crestfallen. No one ignored Daisy's beautiful face. She was always the star of the show. How dare he snub her baby dog?

Today really wasn't having any pity on her ego.

She followed behind him as he walked into the makeshift rooms built around the facility, making the interior of the warehouse look like something out of a movie set.

"We were just using this place for room clearing today," he said, pointing at a spent flash-bang on the floor in the staged living room. "I was going to clean up but decided to wait until you were done."

She nodded. "The more scents, the better. I like to make it hard on her."

He smiled, a *real* full-toothed smile, and he finally looked down at Daisy. "May I touch her?"

Finally, they were getting somewhere.

"Sure," she said, looking at the nameplate on his chest. "Sergeant Anders."

He glanced up at her and looked surprised before connecting the dots with how she would have known his name. "Sorry about being a little short with you," he said, bending the knee to Daisy and petting her.

The animal leaned into him, her bulletproof vest pressing against his. They made quite the pair.

Daisy's butt jiggled as she tried to wag her tail. "She likes you."

At least one of them did. If nothing else, Daisy's endorsement of the man was something to like him for.

"I'm a huge dog guy—it's why I offered to stay behind and help you out."

He had *offered*?

"Well, I appreciate your helping me." She felt suddenly embarrassed that she had taken an instant disliking to him. Maybe she really was too fast to judge.

She would need to focus on her self-improvement for a while.

"What do you need me to do?" he asked, motioning around the place.

She reached into her tactical bag and took out a Ziploc. "This bait has a scent on it. I'll take Daisy outside and make her wait. Then I'm going to need you to take this out of the bag and plant the cloth somewhere in the facility. I don't want to touch it. She knows what I smell like and can use that."

He threw his head back with a laugh. "We'd hate for her to cheat."

"She is smarter than I am sometimes." She smiled.

He looked at her as he stood up, studying her. "I find that hard to believe. The handler is just as important as the dog in K-9 work."

She pushed the bait into his hands and moved to step out the side door before he could read anything on her face. "I'll wait out here."

She felt something in her chest shift as she

walked away from him. Was he hitting on her? Or was she just seeing something that wasn't there because she had been without a man for too long?

Yeah, there was nothing there. She had just witnessed a mirage in the desert of her love life. All she needed was to go on a date with a man, leave in the morning and forget about feelings. Relationships were for people who had the time and patience to deal with them; she had better things to do.

She shifted her weight, like she was readjusting her nonexistent, feelings-proof vest.

"Daisy, you are not a good influence," she said, scratching behind the dog's ears as Daisy looked up at her and gave her a doggie grin. "Like I said. You know what you did, didn't you? You're devious."

Daisy wiggled. "If you want a man in our lives, we can get you a cute dog to run with. Don't you dare look at me and get any kind of silly ideas."

Chapter Two

What a long damned day. He loved training with the special response team, or SRT, but going from 6:00 a.m. until 6:00 p.m. had drained him. When he'd agreed to take care of the K-9 handler, he'd had no idea it was going to be a woman. As soon as she had stepped out of that truck, he'd hated his decision to volunteer even more.

She was way too good-looking, with her long brunette hair pulled back into a loose ponytail and her skintight tactical pants. Looking at her, and the way she moved, he instantly wondered if this woman was here to train or to flirt. He had a history with women who fell in the latter category. He'd met his ex when she had signed up for a ride-along. Things had seemed normal during the ride, but the next day the texting had started, and quicker than he realized, he was in it deep.

Amber had been great—things had been easy

between them—but that had led to most of their problems. She would bow to anything he wanted, with no counterpoints, no opinions of her own and always acquiescence. He had needed a woman who challenged him.

Breaking up with her had been murder. She was nice enough and there was no concrete moment that had torn them apart after two years. It just was...*time*.

She hadn't taken it well and had begged him to stay. He had been tempted to give in—she wasn't a bad girlfriend in any way—but if he was honest, he didn't want to settle for happy enough. He wanted more than that in his life. He wanted a woman who made his heart race when she walked into the room. It sounded stupid, but he wanted a woman who could speak to his soul even in moments when he knew he was wrong and then she could make him right.

But what he was looking for, what he needed, wasn't something he would ever find.

He'd damned well given up looking. And until he figured out what he really wanted, something that made some sense, he wasn't about to jump into a relationship again. He didn't want to hurt anyone because he didn't know what he needed—he was a better man than that, or at least he would have liked to think he was.

Grant walked around the facility, running

scent for Elle and her dog before planting the T-shirt behind a cushion on the floral-patterned couch in the makeshift den. There was probably a better place to hide the smelly thing, but it would have to work. The quicker the dog found what it was looking for and the quicker the beautiful woman and her cute dog were gone, the better.

As he walked back, he reminded himself not to look her in the eyes. If he did, if the little niggle of excitement he felt upon seeing her was truly going to be some kind of feeling, staring into her eyes wasn't going to help. Better to avoid trouble than to walk headfirst into it.

She looked up as he opened the door leading outside. Blue. Her eyes weren't just plain old blue; rather, they were the color of the sky on a summer day—crystal clear and bright, full of spirit.

Damn it. Error. Major error.

"Did you plant the shirt somewhere?" she asked, the question sounding as awkward as he felt.

He nodded. "What else you need me to do?" He squirmed as he stood there, holding the heavy metal door open for her.

"If you want to watch, you can follow us through. But I've got it all from here, or rather… Daisy does," she said, sending him a sexy smile.

Daisy looked up at her, like she realized they were talking about her, and her entire body vibrated with joy. It was as if the dog knew what was going to come and was loving her job. If only everyone on his teams loved their jobs the same way this dog seemed to.

He watched as the woman gave the dog a command in what sounded like Russian.

Though he had worked with K-9 units during SWAT calls, this was one of the few times he had a chance to see what it took to teach the dogs he often saw in action.

He walked behind them as she followed the dog. She wove back and forth, locating the scent. It struck him how different the dog looked from the bouncing, wiggling beast Daisy had been outside to this focused task-driven animal that was now working the room in front of him.

It was impressive.

"I thought most K-9s were German shepherds?"

"Most are, or Belgian Malinois." She didn't look away from Daisy as they worked. "Rotties are somewhat rare in the SRT game, but more common in search and rescue. They are a breed with a peppered track record in the court of public opinion, but they are having a resurgence in popularity."

He heard the words she was saying, but all

he could focus on was the sound of her voice and the way her words were flecked with an accent he couldn't quite put his finger on. She sounded like she was from somewhere farther north, but it wasn't quite Canadian. There was also the twang and hard *A* sounds of the Midwest. Where had she grown up?

Maybe she was a corn-fed girl out of Iowa. Hard raised and strong as hell. It would definitely explain how she had gotten into such a male-dominated field. However, maybe he was wrong—there were more and more women getting into search and rescue, and they were all better for it. The next commander was likely even going to be a woman, Melody Warner. She was as badass as they came in SAR. She could pull together a swift-water rigging quicker and better than any man he knew.

His phone buzzed, and he ignored it, though he knew it was likely something to do with work.

"How did you get involved with rottweilers?" he asked, trying to ignore the pull to answer his work phone—it should have been priority number one, but all he could focus on was her and this place and how she smelled like floral perfumes and rubber dog toys.

"My best friend runs Big Sky Rottweiler Rescue. They focus on rehoming rotts who have been surrendered or abandoned to shelters." She rushed after Daisy, who was pulling hard on the leather lead as they made their way down the hall. "Daisy came to me after living in a cage for over a year."

He looked at the beautiful, healthy dog who was sniffing the ground like it held all the answers.

His phone buzzed again, an angry bee just looking to lance his flesh. "Excuse me for a minute." He lifted a finger, knowing she would go about her business though all he wanted her to do was stay by his side and continue his time with her. Being here, watching her work and just learning the steps was the break he needed from his day.

And yet, life called.

"Hello?" he asked, turning away for a moment and walking toward the main door.

"You're working with Elle Spade right now, correct?" He instinctively glanced in her direction as the sheriff spoke.

"Yeah, why?"

"Tell her that there has been an incident… involving one Lily Clark and her family." The sheriff paused, clearing his throat. "I have also approved your volunteer SAR team to act on this one."

"What are you talking about? What happened?" And why would he be asked to tell Elle about it? He was having a hard time pulling the real meaning together behind the sheriff's cryptic instructions.

"A three-year-old girl, Lily Clark, and her mother, Catherine, have gone missing. It looks as though there was some kind of altercation inside the residence, but the team is still sorting through everything. I have yet to get the full report from the crime scene." Grant heard the clink of ice in a glass, but he wouldn't dare ask the sheriff if he had been drinking—such questions only led to lies or trouble. "We aren't sure what happened to the mother, but we have reason to believe the little girl slipped out of her house and may be lost in the national forest service land that abuts their property. Both are, as of yet, unaccounted for."

"I'll pull together my team, and we will head out there as soon as possible."

"Sooner than that. I need you out there now. Go grab Elle and get in your truck. Head straight there and let your team take care of everything else. If you need me to call in one of the coordinators to help, I can."

That wasn't procedure, and he couldn't make sense of why the sheriff would be pushing him like this when he damned well knew that everything SAR did was done as quickly and safely as possible—not only for those they were sent to rescue or recover but also for all members of the unit.

"Yeah, call in Commander Warner. She is the best team leader we've got. But can I ask why the push?"

The sheriff sighed. "Lily Clark isn't just an average kid. She is United States Senator Dean Clark's daughter. If we don't get that girl back…" The sheriff trailed off.

He didn't need to explain that the senator controlled much of their funding—or lack thereof. If a senator turned against them, they would be limited to nothing more than donations and fundraising events.

Basically, if they failed…so did their program.

As awful as that might be, though, it didn't compare to the situation at hand—a missing girl, probably frightened beyond imagining.

"I'll be there as quickly as I can. Text me the address. You make the call to Warner. Get her up to speed. Out." He hung up his phone, remembering that he hadn't even asked the sheriff why he was supposed to tell Elle about the girl's disappearance. Hell, it was probably so she could bring the dog.

He ran down the hall. "Hey, Elle, SAR got a call!"

She stepped out of the makeshift den, Daisy holding a rubber ball in her mouth and wiggling while Elle pushed the T-shirt he'd hidden back into the Ziploc bag. "Do whatever you need to. I can lock up here. Seriously, and thank you for letting us train with you."

His face puckered. "Actually, the sheriff just called personally. He knew you were here and asked that you go with me on this one."

"Really? Why?" She cocked her head, an oddly canine mannerism, but it fit the woman.

"Do you know the Clarks?" he asked, his stomach clenching, though he wasn't sure exactly why. "Lily and Catherine?"

She stared at him, unmoving and unblinking, as though her world had just come crashing down. Daisy stopped moving and looked up at Elle like she could feel the change in the energy around the woman just as abruptly as he did. The dog sank to the floor, laying her head on Elle's feet and letting the ball fall from her mouth and roll haphazardly over the concrete.

"What happened to her?" Elle asked, her voice sounding breathless as all the color drained from her features.

It was strange, but he could understand the dog's sudden need to touch her, to comfort her in the only way possible. And yet he barely knew this woman or why this news would affect her so dramatically. "Something has happened up at their place, some kind of altercation."

"What kind of *altercation*?" She spat the word.

"I can't tell you." He moved to touch her, but she jerked away. "Are you going to be okay?"

She rushed past him, bumping hard against him like she had somehow forgotten he was there even though he had been speaking to her.

Daisy ran behind her as they sprinted outside.

As he stood there, he could make out the sound of her truck revving to life and her tires squealing on the asphalt. As quickly as the woman nosed her way into his life, she had sprinted out of it—and he was far more confused than ever. In a matter of minutes, he'd gone from safely contained and tired from a long day, to geared up and having his and his team's asses on the chopping block…and it seemed highly likely it was all because of her and secrets he was yet to discover.

Chapter Three

The entire ride back to the Clarks', Elle couldn't think of anything except Lily. She'd only been missing a matter of hours, and already things had gone haywire. She should never have left the little girl.

Hopefully the altercation Grant had alluded to was nothing more than a fistfight, nothing involving weapons. She should have asked Grant more questions. If only she had been thinking. That was always one of her biggest and most profound faults—emotions and actions first, questions later. It wasn't a recipe for success in her personal or professional life.

She grabbed her phone. She could call him. But as she looked at the screen, she realized she didn't have his number. *Damn it.*

No doubt, if she had been able to talk to him, he would be unlikely to give her much. He'd been pretty vague with providing any sort of details, and when it came to law enforcement and anyone in special operations, she had learned long ago that when they kept silent, it was for a reason.

That silence was always chilling.

Her mind went to all the dark places as she sped down the road. Lily had to be okay. Catherine could fend for herself—well, so long as the altercation was as minor as she hoped. Yet why would the sheriff ask for her to come if it was something inconsequential?

Perhaps it was so she could act as a witness. Or maybe they needed her there to help Lily calm down. Maybe the little girl was asking for her.

She smiled faintly at the thought. Of course, that was probably it. Otherwise the sheriff would probably not even know Elle existed.

Then again, Grant had first told her that *SAR had a call*. That meant search and rescue teams were involved. Which meant that one or both of the Clark ladies were missing. It was probably Lily. Maybe Lily was just playing, hiding away in some closet in the house and Catherine couldn't find her.

Yes, this was probably all blown out of proportion and Elle was just jumping to the darkness out of habit—she and her military contracting teams had spent far too many nights planted in the tumultuous and dangerous world of war-ravaged countries.

Her mind drifted to Afghanistan. They had been running an operation for the military-contracted agency, or MCA, she'd been working for at the time, taking her dog into the mud houses and working to clear them of explosives. In the Pashtun region, none of the dwellings were for single families. Rather, extended family groups crowded into them, and they normally held between twelve and twenty people. Most of the residents hated dogs and Americans and, with her having both strikes against her, she was never a welcome sight—not to mention she was a woman working in an area heavy with Taliban forces.

On her last trip, she had been operating in a building that had already had one IED detonation in the courtyard. When she'd arrived on scene, the team before her had pulled out all the remaining living members of the family. The complex had taken on an eerie, disquieting feel that spoke of the horror that had filled it only hours before her arrival.

It wasn't the first time she had been to a place like that, where the acrid scent of spent explosives still mixed with the tang of freshly spilled blood and lingered in the air like a eulogy, yet when she got to the courtyard, she hadn't been prepared for the scene that had unfolded.

She had to work through a number of bodies, most so thoroughly peppered with shrapnel that if it weren't for their clothes, it would have been hard to tell if they were women or men. There was a small crater where the initial blast had happened. There, at the edge, was a well-worn pair of children's Adidas sneakers. One was tipped on its side, as if the kid who had been wearing them had been blown out of them.

She later learned that, according to eyewitnesses, the child had picked up the bomb and had been playing with it when it detonated.

She'd been shipped out later that week and had never been happier to get out of a country.

It had taken her a long time after her feet had arrived on American soil for her soul to come home, as well. No matter how many debriefings or offers to speak to chaplains happened, she would never again go to sleep without the image of those shoes popping into the front of her mind.

Ever since that day, she'd been on a mission to be on the front line when it came to children and her job. Most would have backed away, put distance between themselves and the possible horrors that would hurt them the most, but not her. It was odd, but seeing those horrors made her want to do everything in her power to never have those tragedies or hellscapes happen again—and therefore witnessed by anyone else.

She could be the whipping girl so others wouldn't have to endure the same traumas.

Trauma. Her past. All of it was swirling into her mind and masking the reality of her present. She couldn't let that happen. Not now. Not when Lily was likely in trouble.

Maybe it was the trauma that scared her the most, nothing more than the ghosts of the past haunting the present. More than likely, Lily was probably just being Lily and hiding in the house somewhere, she reminded herself. Maybe her father had called in the cavalry when really only patience and steadiness were all that were needed.

Maybe this was nothing more than the senator pulling strings in order to bring the media to their knees at his beck and call—attention to him and his family, especially in their time of need, would likely be helpful in any sort of political campaign. Hell, he was known for pandering to the media.

If this was some kind of political move, she was going to have to quit the job on the spot. Then again, she couldn't leave Lily alone and unsupervised with two such toxic people.

As she crested the top of the hill, she turned

down the driveway that led to the Clarks'. The place was lit up with a collection of red and blue lights. The image made her stomach drop. In the evening shadows, the lights reflected off the snow and made it look like some sort of scene out of a murder documentary.

Murder.

No.

There was no way Lily could be dead.

Yet the scene made it clear that this situation was far more serious than what she had been hoping to find.

As she pulled up the driveway, her thoughts moved to the men who had been standing around in the living room like frat boys when she had been here earlier.

Was she here because of something they did? It wouldn't have surprised her if things had escalated into a full-blown altercation with that kind of crowd. When there was a room full of self-important and power-hungry men drinking and smoking cigars, no doubt they would have been trying to one-up each other. They were probably playing at the hierarchy of asshats.

For now, she just needed to get the information she required and go to work in helping Lily. She couldn't go down the road of what-ifs and hows. She was here to help, first and foremost. The rest of the professionals on-site could help her make sense of everything else. It was the reason they had teams. And, in her case, she not only had the crew that was already swarming around the house, but her family, as well.

Whatever the police couldn't handle—or were limited in what they could legally do—her family and teams at STEALTH could step in and take care of. It was one of the best things about her job and family. She was always surrounded by badasses. In fact, some could have even said she was one, but if she was, it was because of her dog. If she had to pick the biggest badass in her family, the title would have to go to her sister, Kendra.

She parked, got out of her truck and walked to the back door to check on Daisy. Grant pulled in behind her, a sour expression on his face. As he exited his truck, the look on his face deepened. "Don't you think you were driving a little fast?" From the tone of his voice, she would have thought he was kidding, but from his expression he was clearly annoyed.

"If Lily is in trouble, there's no speed limit in the world that's going to keep me from getting to her." She gave Daisy a scratch behind the ears as the dog stared at her and attempted to make sense of everything that was happening.

"So, you do know this girl?" Grant asked. "I mean, I assumed you did...given the fact you ran away from me like your ass was on fire. But you could have at least let me give you the lay of the land before you tore out."

She huffed. He wasn't wrong. "Yes, I know Lily. I was hired as her guard by her family. I only left here a few hours ago." She clicked Daisy's lead onto her collar, readying her for whatever their next steps may be. "What's happened to her?"

His sour, annoyed expression was quickly replaced with one of a pained empathy. "From what I was able to glean on the ride over, the mother and her child have gone missing. They initially believed the little girl may have slipped out of the house sometime after you left...but the scene's—"

"Lily didn't sneak out of the house," she said, interrupting him. "Lily isn't that kind of girl." Her thoughts came in a mad dash.

"I know, but—"

"If anyone is at fault here, it isn't Lily. Her parents are..." She glanced up at the front door of the house. The senator was nowhere to be seen. "They are not as *attentive* to Lily as parents should be. In fact, I'm surprised they didn't have a nanny on staff. They should have."

Catherine and Dean hadn't been especially forthcoming with why they had hired Elle and her team to watch over Lily, but if they thought there was enough of a security threat that they needed to call in private VIP teams, then obviously there was something going on.

She should have pushed for more answers before taking this job. She should have gotten all the details. And yet, they had been vague. In a world of shadows, she hadn't found it surprising at the time. Maybe it had been their hubris or hers, but as long as she was around, she hadn't been overly concerned that anything bad would happen to Lily. But that had been on the condition that she was around. This had happened after her watch had ended. She should have been adamant about making sure that Lily had around-the-clock coverage. Or at least that they had boots on the ground outside the house.

She looked at Grant. He'd crossed his arms over his chest and was looking down at his feet, and she realized that she had once again spoken over him. When would she just start listening instead of pushing her way through life?

"Sorry. So, both Catherine and Lily are missing?" Elle asked, more focused on the child than the mother. At least Catherine could look out for herself.

He nodded. "No one knows where they went, but there was a sign of a struggle inside the residence. A table is broken and, from what the deputy on the inside said, there were shots fired within the house, and a gun registered to Catherine was found under a sofa. It was a .38 Special, and they believe it is the same caliber as that which left the holes in the walls."

"So you believe Catherine was shooting at someone?"

Grant shrugged. "Hard to say how this played out as of now. We are pretty early on in our investigation. You know how these things have a way of distorting under first impressions."

He spoke to her as though someone had filled him in on some key details of her life, but she couldn't imagine who or when. She had always been insistent about keeping herself to herself, but then again, this was Montana.

"One of the neighbors said they saw you leaving the house this afternoon," he continued. "It is believed you were one of the last people in or out of the house."

"What? No. I wasn't the last one here by any means. There were quite a few men in the living room, socializing with Mrs. Clark, when I left. But, wait…"

He didn't call her here to help in the search. No. He'd called her here because she was one of their possible suspects.

"Am I a suspect in their disappearance?" she asked.

If she had been the lead working this case,

she would have been her first stop, too. And it had been one hell of a play for Grant to bring her right to this place and put her on the spot, when, in fact, he was really questioning her. She had fallen for his game hook, line and sinker.

But she wasn't afraid—she had nothing to hide.

"I didn't say anything of the sort," he said. "However, what time did you leave here?" Grant asked, careful to phrase his questions in a way that if she hadn't been aware she was being interrogated, she wouldn't have picked up on it.

"I left about thirty minutes before I met up with you." She scowled. "I know what you're thinking, but I'm telling you right now that if there was anything or any information I could give you about this little girl's disappearance, I'd be the first to do it."

Grant twitched. "You're always two steps ahead, aren't you?"

"I just live in this world, one of law enforcement and carefully constructed realities."

He chuckled. "I do appreciate that we have the ability to speak the same language on this." He seemed to relax, whatever suspicions he held about her momentarily falling to the wayside.

He was trying to play her again, to make her feel comfortable around him in an attempt to get more information. Little did he know, she was a master at that stupid game. However, it was odd and uncomfortable for her to be sitting on the receiving end.

"Do your guys know how long they've been missing? Who called this in?"

He leaned against the front of her truck. Daisy whined at her, and she stroked her head.

"Again, I don't have all the details, but I think it was a neighbor who reported hearing gunshots."

"Any blood?" She clicked off Daisy's lead and closed the back door of the truck, leaving the dog safely tucked inside. "Did your guys look everywhere for Lily? That girl won't just answer to anyone. If she's hiding in there, she's probably not going to come out for anyone other than someone she knows." She took a step toward the house.

"Stop," Grant said, putting his hands up to keep her from advancing. "I know what you are thinking, but you can't just barge into that house and start yelling for Lily. This is potentially an active crime scene. Whatever we do, we have to be careful. We have to follow procedure, at least as much as we can."

Her hands were balled into tight fists, almost like her body wanted to strike out and take down anything and anyone who stood be-

tween her and Lily's safety—or lack thereof—
even if that someone was the sergeant.

She tried to control her impulses to run into
the house and flip open every cabinet and over-
turn every drawer in her search for Lily, but it
was a struggle. Daisy whined from the back
seat, and when Elle glanced over at her, Daisy
barked.

I know. I screwed up, Daisy, she thought. *I
never should have left today. I knew something
wasn't right. I effing knew it.*

Daisy's nose pressed on the glass, and she
whined again.

She should have trusted her gut and not left
when she had seen the men in the house alone
with Catherine. She should have taken Lily
and gone somewhere…anywhere. And yet, she
hadn't listened to the little voice, and now her
ward and her mother were missing.

She thought about Gavin de Becker's *The Gift
of Fear.* Like so many other self-help and self-
defense–themed books, it spoke of a person's
intuition being their greatest weapon in their
defense arsenal. There was nothing more effective to defer crime and injuries than to avoid
situations that put a person at risk. Yet the only
person who had avoided anything was Elle—
she had wanted to avoid a confrontation with
Catherine, and in the end…

Her boss was nowhere to be found.

One confrontation and she could have saved a woman and a child from disappearing.

Elle had avoided conflict and walked them straight into danger.

Maybe she needed to read that book again. Then again, she didn't need a book to tell her to be afraid. She knew all too much about that on her own.

"Would you mind taking me through the house? I won't touch anything, but if we are going to look for Lily, I'm going to need to know where we are going to have to start." *And whether or not she is still alive.*

"Why don't we leave Daisy for now? I want to do a quick walk-through and then, if you feel it necessary, we can have her do a sweep. Okay?" Grant asked, giving her a pinched, pleading look.

She opened the back door and clicked Daisy's lead in place and then helped her step out of the back. "Dog goes. In a case like this, I can promise you that she is likely to pull more information than we ever could. Humans are always at the dumb end of the lead."

Chapter Four

The house still smelled like it had when she left, a strange mix of whiskey, expensive women's perfume and cigar smoke. Now, however, beneath the familiar odors was the distinct scent that came with the police—disinfectant, sweat, leather and gun powder.

She lifted her shirt, taking a quick sniff to see which world she smelled of after being in the training warehouse, but all she could smell was this morning's shower, fresh air and Daisy.

Careful to slip under the tape, she walked into the foyer and glanced into the living room. The various law officers were in other parts of the house now, so the room was empty. "When I left, Catherine was here with a group of about eight men." Daisy sat down beside her, leaning against her, her body tight and ready for action.

"Do you happen to know the identity of any of those men? Or what they were doing here?" Sergeant Anders asked.

She shook her head. "This family has a lot of foot traffic in and out of the place. It's why I normally take Lily out of the house when she is under my care. It is easier to control the variables."

"Are you saying that the type of people who came through this place weren't who you would call reliable and safe?" he asked, reaching for his pocket like he wanted to take notes, but then he stopped and dropped his hands back down to his sides.

"It's not that they were drugged-out meth heads, or people who you would look at and think they were dangerous—actually, far from it. These people weren't the kind to keep themselves in bad company. Their lives were completely taken up by their image and the public's opinion of that image. Especially right now, as the senator is up for reelection and is behind in the polls."

She looked at the spot where she had last seen the stranger in khakis who had been smoking the cigar. Aside from the broken side table and three bullet holes in the wall to her right, nothing was out of place. If anything, it was too clean. Had someone staged this?

Grant bent over slightly and pointed toward the couch. "Right there, see the gun?" He pointed in the direction he was looking.

She crouched down. There, on the floor under the couch, was the .38 Special. She didn't recognize the gun, but she hadn't even been aware that Catherine owned a gun, let alone kept it at the ready.

"This room is ridiculously clean," Grant said, standing up. "Do the Clarks hire a cleaning staff?"

The question seemed kind of out of place, but she assumed he must have been thinking the same about the lack of detritus and debris in what they had been told was the site of an altercation that may or may not have led to Lily and Catherine going missing.

"Yes, but they only come in once a week," she said.

"Did Mrs. Clark always keep house in such a way?"

She stood up and chuckled. "Everything about the Clarks was always picture-perfect. I agree that this isn't much to work with for investigators, but… Who knows?" She shrugged, trying to dispel some of her nerves. "This whole thing may not be as bad as we first assumed. Did your people try and call Catherine? Dean?"

Grant gave her a look that would have crumbled a lesser woman. "Yes, we tried to contact Catherine and Dean. Dean is unavailable. We have the Washington, DC, police department looking for him in order to notify him about what has happened. And Catherine's phone was found in the backyard—its screen was cracked, but we have bagged it for evidence and our teams will see if they can pull any information." He started to walk again, and she followed after, Daisy close at her heels.

"Were you and Mrs. Clark close?" Grant asked, looking over at her with a sidelong glance.

She shook her head as they made their way toward the back of the house. "Hardly. I'm nothing more than an employee. In fact, today she tried to give me a hundred-dollar tip. It was her way of reminding me that I'm nothing to Lily other than paid help—not a friend, not a parent and definitely not someone irreplaceable."

Grant reached up and touched her shoulder, the motion far too real and sympathetic than she was prepared for. He didn't need to say he was sorry; she could see it on him, and she didn't like it.

"It's okay. Sometimes it is good to be reminded to keep a little emotional distance from your work. And, regardless of how much I enjoyed Lily, I needed to keep in mind that the care of her was a job." Yet, even talking about what the girl *shouldn't* have meant to her made her ache with concern.

"Do you feel like you failed at that job?" he asked, almost as though he could read her truths on her features.

A lump formed in her throat, and she knew if she spoke, her voice would crack with pain. She simply shrugged.

"No matter what, Elle, you didn't fail this girl. You did exactly what you were paid to do during your working hours."

Had she? Her gaze moved to the travertine floor and the beige-and-gray speckling of its glistening surface; in her few months here she had never noticed the way it flowed like water.

He sighed. "I can see you are just like me. When you're off the clock, you struggle to leave the job at the doorstep. I know what that's like. And I know what you're likely struggling with. But you can't do this to yourself."

"My guilt will subside when I know that Lily is safe—and her mother."

He opened his mouth and then shut it, but she knew what he was going to say…that they both needed to be prepared for any possible outcomes.

As they walked by the stairs, she pointed in the direction of the living quarters. "Do you want me to show you Lily's room? Maybe there is something there." Really, though, she was just hoping that as soon as she stepped into the room, Lily would come bounding out from inside her closet or from under her bed; she loved to play hide-and-seek.

Even as she considered it, she could feel in her gut that such a thing wasn't going to happen. Lily wasn't in this house. There were at least twenty different law enforcement personnel circulating through the residence, taking pictures and documenting the scene. Several were talking on their phones, and their voices mixed into an odd cacophony of stoic babble and garbled calls from dispatch on handsets.

He started up the stairs, and she stepped around him, leading him down the long white-carpeted hallway toward the girl's bedroom. "I could never understand why anyone in their right mind would have carpet this color when they have children. Since I've been here, they've already had to replace the carpet in Lily's bedroom once after she spilled a glass of grape juice—organic, of course."

He smirked. "I can't profess to understand or comprehend the thought processes of the extremely wealthy."

"It's wasteful." As she spoke, she realized that she had completely unleashed all of the opinions and judgments she had been withholding.

Yet, with the sergeant, it may not have been the wisest of choices.

She needed to shut up. All he needed to know were facts that would help them locate Lily and Catherine. Everything else was frivolous.

The window where she had last seen Lily was open, and the cold winter air crept through the little girl's bedroom. It sent a chill down Elle's back, but she wasn't sure if it was because of the cold or the fear of what the window being open could have meant.

By the window, on the corner of the ledge, was a Barbie doll, her hair half-shorn and the other colored pink with Magic Marker. If Catherine had seen such a doll, it would have been pitched in the garbage and replaced with a new doll, hair intact.

"Lily was sitting there," she said, pointing at the ledge. "She waved at me when I left, then I came to see you."

"After Catherine gave you the tip?" Grant asked.

She gave him the side-eye.

"I'm just making sure that I'm tracking all of this correctly."

"Yes, after Catherine slipped me the money. I still have it." She reached down toward her pocket, but he waved her off. "Why do I get the feeling you are struggling to trust me?"

"I don't rush into anything, especially trusting people I just met—even in law enforcement. Don't be offended. It's not a reflection on you."

Was that this guy's way of telling her he was all kinds of screwed up? He'd hardly be the first LEO she'd met with a chip on his shoulder and a need for therapy. In fact, it was so normal, that she was forced to wonder if it was a chicken-or-the-egg kind of conundrum. On the other hand, perhaps the same could be said of her.

Beside the bed she spotted the wing-tip shoes, the ones with the black around the tops, that Lily had been wearing when she'd left. They were askew, pitched exactly where the little girl must have taken them off. No other shoes were missing, making her wonder what Lily was wearing. She couldn't have been out of the house. Not in this weather, not without shoes.

Then again, that was assuming she had been taken out willingly. If that little girl was out there in the cold, whoever had her would have hell to pay. *If* someone had her.

GRANT'S HANDSET CRACKLED to life. "Officer 466, we have blood. Requesting backup." He recognized Deputy Terrill's voice.

Pressing the button on his handset, he leaned into the mic. "Ten-four, location?"

"Four sixty-six, we've located it just outside the property line to the south," Deputy Terrill said.

Grant glanced over at Elle, whose eyes were wide and filled with fear. Blood was never a positive sign, but at least they had something to help them find the missing Clarks. Yet, he couldn't help but wonder if including Elle on this one was going to be too much for the woman. "Elle, if you don't want to come with me, you don't have to. You are welcome to stick around here with one of the other officers and help them look around the house and see if you can pull more evidence."

Elle shook her head violently. "There's no way I'm not going to be involved on this. But let me get Daisy ready. She knows Lily's scent." She patted the dog's head.

He smiled. She was right. This dog was probably their best bet in tracking down the woman and child. "Go for it. I'll meet you around back." Her jaw was set, and where there had once been fear in her eyes, the look was now replaced with rage. He could understand it. "Again, Elle, if you change your mind about going along, all you have to do is let me know—we can get another handler in here. Sometimes when we're too close to a case, it can take a lot out of us."

"It's far harder on me knowing that Lily and Catherine are out there somewhere, possibly hurt, and I'm doing nothing about it. There's not a chance in hell I'm going to change my mind."

ELLE AND HER dog walked out of the bedroom, but she looked back one more time as if she hoped that she would spot the little girl hiding somewhere in a corner or behind a drape, when they both knew all too well what the likely outcome was in a case like this.

He waited a few minutes, looking for anything out of place—a hair band, blood spatter, even an empty glass. But the only thing that seemed slightly out of place was the little girl's shoes. Clearly Lily had been in a hurry when she'd removed them. Just from the way they were strewn on the floor, he could almost tell the child's personality—it was the only part of the room that really spoke of the little girl and not her mother.

Elle had made a point of telling him that the family was definitely the kind who would keep everything in line. Which made him wonder exactly how the Clarks had found themselves in this kind of predicament. Then again, sometimes when people held on too tight, it was because they were the ones who had the most to fear if they lost control. He knew a little bit about that—he always felt as if he was one hairbreadth away from disaster, both in his personal life and his professional one.

As he made his way out of Lily's bedroom, he walked past the master bedroom. From inside, he could hear a few officers talking about the senator in colorful language. As their sergeant, he should have stuck his head into the room and reminded the team that it was more than possible that one of them had their cameras rolling and everything they were saying was likely being recorded, but he didn't bother. They had already been warned they were always being monitored. At this point, if they wanted to talk smack about the senator, he wasn't going to be the one who put his ass on the line to stop them.

Then again, crap always rolled downhill, and if he didn't speak up, this could well end up with him standing at attention in the chief's office and taking a tongue-lashing for not keeping his team in line during a high-priority call.

He opened the door without announcing his presence. The three officers standing near the end of the bed glanced up at him with guilty looks, and the deputy on the left put his hand up in a slight wave. "How's it going, Sarge? You find anything?"

The deputy next to him had a slight redness to his cheeks. They all knew they had been caught.

"I'm sure I don't need to tell you how important this case could be for our department. I recommend you guys get your asses in gear and do everything in our power to find these missing females and all while not running our mouths." He pointed at the camera that he had attached to his vest.

All nodded, reminding him of three little monkeys—no see, no hear, no speak. He didn't care if they had to tap the message on the floor to one another, just so long as they fully understood that it was truly all their asses on the line here.

If they didn't get the Clarks back into their custody quick, fast and in a hurry, the media would blow this all up and they would be the ones taking the most flak. No doubt, as team leader, he would be made out to be a Barney Fife—some bumbling cop from a bygone era who didn't always know his ass from his elbow.

Yeah, he couldn't run the risk of those girls being gone for any more time than absolutely necessary.

Without so much as a backhanded wave, he rushed out of the bedroom and downstairs, nearly jogging as he made it outside.

A group of team members was standing outside the white vinyl fence, the kind that looked beautiful but was brittle and prone to shattering in the cold. The snow was deeper in the back of the house, and it crunched under his feet as he was careful to walk in areas not taped off. Perpetrators' footprints could be on the ground.

Deputy Terrill looked over at him and gave him a tip of the head in acknowledgment as he said something to the other two officers he was standing with.

Daisy popped out from around the side of the house, her nose already to the ground as she wove back and forth, working over the scene. Her black tail stood at attention as she moved toward him and Elle came into view.

He stood watching the dog move right and left, huffing as she took in the cold winter air and picked apart the medley of odors that must have been peppering it. He'd always heard a dog's sense of smell was at least a thousand times keener than a human's, which meant Daisy could probably pick up everything that had happened in the house today…all the people who had walked through its doors and even the cars they had driven in. Hell, she probably could make out the scent of the discarded fast-food wrappers and chewed gum that were in the garbage bags inside the people's cars.

Having that kind of ability to make out scents

was an incredible superpower, but what made it even more incredible was that these dogs and their handlers had also managed to create a system of communication through training that enabled them to understand what the other was looking for and when it was found. He had seen the K-9 units work before. He'd even been asked to take a bite during training—and he would only do that once. He had tremendous respect for the human-animal bonds that allowed these teams to do their jobs effectively.

Elle finally looked up from Daisy as the dog slowed. He met her gaze, and there was an intensity in her eyes that made it clear she was just as on-task as the dog. Yet, as he looked at her, he couldn't manage the same level of professionalism—all he could think about was the brunette hair that had fallen free of her messy bun and was cascading down her neck. She had a slender neck that curved delicately into the arch of her shoulder. The notch at the base of her throat was exposed, and sitting at its center was a diamond on a gold chain.

The place where her necklace rested looked soft, kissably soft. If he kissed her there, was she the kind of woman who would tip her head back and moan, or was she the type to pull in a breath and tighten in anticipation? If he had to guess, she held her breath. She didn't seem like the kind of woman who would melt easily under a man's touch.

The thought of another man touching her made the hairs on the back of his neck rise.

He turned away from them, forcing himself to work. This wasn't the time. Actually, it was never going to be a good time to think about her the way he was thinking about her and all the things he would like to do to her body.

"Sergeant Anders, over here," Terrill said, motioning toward something on the ground.

He made his way over to Terrill as Daisy worked a weaving path across the backyard. He didn't know what scent Elle had put her on, but from the way the dog moved, he couldn't help but wonder if it was some small, skittish mammal—the scent path moved like a rabbit.

Careful to keep in the trail the officers had already created in the snow, he slipped between the rails of the fence and came to a stop beside Terrill. "What's going on? You found blood?"

Terrill pointed at the ground a few feet out from where the men stood. There, the snow had been trampled down and there was a mess of small footprints. It looked as though someone had lain in the snow and rolled around, but it was hard to tell the size of the individual— even if it was an adult or a child. Yet, at the edge of the compressed snow was a splatter of blood. The holes the warm blood had created in the snow were dime sized, and if the holes hadn't been edged in the pinkish-red stain, it would have been almost impossible to see. It definitely wasn't a quantity of blood that would mean whomever it had belonged to was close to death, but that was the only good news.

Daisy whined from behind him, and he turned and watched as she slipped under the fence and moved toward them. She pulled on her lead, the muscles in her shoulders pressing out hard as she tried to force Elle to come where she wanted her. Elle stopped, holding Daisy back.

"Sidet," Elle commanded in Russian.

Daisy dropped to her haunches, sitting. There was no moment of hesitation, no pause between command and obedient action.

When he'd been a kid, they'd had a chocolate Lab. The dog, Duke, would only listen to him when and if it was beneficial to the dog. He couldn't even begin to imagine how much these two must have worked and trained to get to the perfection of that simple command.

She was definitely capable of a level of dedication that he envied. He had always thought himself good at his job, but the officers under his command weren't nearly as well trained.

Maybe he needed to start giving them treats and praise.

He smirked, but it disappeared as he noticed the terror in Elle's eyes as she looked at the droplets of blood in the snow.

"Can you tell us whose blood that is?" he asked, afraid that he knew the answer before he had even asked the question.

She chewed on her bottom lip for a quick second. "I had Daisy on Lily's scent, but that doesn't necessarily mean that blood belongs to her. If there was someone out here with her, it could be theirs," she said, but he could hear the feeble hope in her tone.

Elle stepped around the bloodstain and moved toward the timber. He followed a few feet behind her, letting her and the dog do their work. There were two sets of tracks in the snow, what looked like a man's and a woman's. Their footfalls were wide apart, as if they had been running.

She stopped after about twenty yards and turned to him. "Look."

The footsteps in the snow appeared to grow closer, like the man and woman had slowed down and then come to a full stop. Where they had stopped was another set of small footprints—complete with toe marks. At the center of one of the child's footprints was a pink smudge, as though she had blood on her bare-footed step.

Lily was in far more danger than either of them had assumed.

Chapter Five

The wind had kicked up as the sun was touching the tips of the mountains to the west; snow was fluttering down, and with each passing minute it seemed to be coming down faster in plump, wet flakes. If they didn't work quickly, soon the easy trail would be obscured and they would have to rely solely on Daisy's nose.

She tried to quell her disgust as she looked at the marks in the snow where Lily had been dragging her bare feet.

Who in their right mind would have brought a three-year-old out into the cold and then made her walk barefooted in the snow?

When she found the kidnapper, she would personally make sure they hiked twice as far without their goddamned shoes—and that was *if* Lily was okay. If she was hurt, or if her little feet were frostbitten, there would be more than hell to pay.

Is there something worse than hell? She paused

at the thought but followed Daisy as the dog moved ahead.

All she knew was that anyone who hurt Lily would suffer pain at her hands that would be real and unbearable. It was more than possible that she would be the one who ended up in jail, but if she got justice for Lily, it would be worth it.

Her jaw ached as she jogged with Daisy, and she realized that she had been gritting her teeth, though for how long, she didn't know.

There was another long drag mark in the snow where it appeared as though Lily had literally stopped walking and had been pulled ahead.

That a girl. At least her friend was putting up a fight.

Since she had been taking care of Lily, she had been spending time having the kiddo do simple exercises—jumping jacks and push-ups, squats and lunges. At the time, Elle had been using the exercise as something to do to keep Lily busy, but now she was glad she had helped the girl gain strength. Though, never in her wildest dreams had she thought the child would need the stamina and strength they had been working to build for surviving the elements.

Thankfully, she hadn't spotted any more blood

in the snow. If it was Lily who had been bleeding, she was going to survive…probably.

If only she had some kind of idea why they were out here, what had made them disappear into the woods. Was the man with them keeping guard, or had he taken them? Were they running or being forced to run?

Her mind went wild with a million different theories, playing them out from start to finish. Though it was good for her to be prepared and to try to make sense of what had happened, she wasn't a detective; she was merely a private security contractor, and she couldn't rush to any conclusions. If she assumed anything, it could adversely affect their tracking and Grant's team's investigation. Well, *her* opinions and assumptions wouldn't affect them, or at least she didn't think they would; they seemed like a team that had their roles and expectations dialed in.

She could make out the sounds of his footfalls crunching in the snow beside her, and she glanced over at him. The red light on Grant's body camera was on, indicating he was recording everything they were doing. *Good*.

If they missed anything, or if something unexpected happened, he would have a record of it. Maybe they could find things after the fact when they were back in their warm offices and reviewing the recordings. Though, if she had her way, there would be no need. She wouldn't be stopping her search until Lily was safely back in her care and out of harm's way.

The mountain grew steeper and, as the sun slipped behind the peaks and cast them in the cold, wintery shade of impending night, the trail they had been following became harder and harder to see. As she wove around a bend in what must have been a game trail under the snow, the footsteps they'd been following disappeared. For a moment, she stopped and waited for Grant to catch up. He was saying something into his handset, and as he stopped beside her, he struggled to catch his breath.

She would have assumed a sergeant would be in better shape—he must have spent his entire adult life getting to the position he was in within the department. Yet he probably was more of a paper pusher than a boots-on-the-ground kind of guy. It was one of the benefits from moving up in any organization—manual labor grew lighter while mental fortitude became more pivotal.

"You okay?" he asked, letting out a long breath as though he was forcing his body to fall back in line with his hard-edged spirit.

She nodded. "The trail just disappeared."

He looked down at the ground, seeming to

notice it for the first time in at least a mile. "You're right." He glanced up at the sky, and a fat snowflake landed on his cheek. As he looked back toward her, she watched as the flake disappeared into nothing more than a droplet of water, which he wiped away with the back of his hand.

Even in the gray, she could see his cheeks were cherry red from the cold and exertion. She considered slowing down for him, allowing him time to recover, but there was no time for rest. Not when it came to Lily. They had to go.

"Hasn't Daisy been leading us, not you?" he asked.

She shook her head. "Yeah, but no. We've mostly been just following the tracks. The problem with snow and cold is that in this kind of weather, especially with the wind, the scents she uses to track can disappear pretty rapidly. The wind alone can really make the odors drift off course. That being said, I'll put her on this, but if they got off this trail, it could really slow down our progress."

He gave a dip of the head, and though she thought he would have been secretly relieved to slow down, he looked as frustrated as she felt. "We won't stop, Elle, I promise. I will do everything and put every resource I can behind finding Lily." His handset crackled, and she could make out a woman's voice but couldn't hear what she was saying. A thin smile moved over his lips and he looked up at her. "Search and rescue is on the ground. They just arrived at the house."

She glanced down at her watch. They had been on the trail now for a little under an hour. At the pace they had been moving, that made them just less than three miles from where Lily had last been seen.

"They are putting together their plan, but for now it sounds like they are going to bring up their four-wheelers, then send hikers out to catch up with us, maybe even get Two Bear helicopter to fly them in, but they are still working on that. I let them know we are still running tracks, but that the tracks may have given out."

A thin wave of relief washed over her. At the very least, they wouldn't be the only two on the mountain searching.

She gave Daisy her command, and the dog got on scent. Daisy pulled at the leather lead, glad to finally be back in control of the situation. The rocks under the slick pack of snow made travel slippery as they moved higher and deeper into the timber. The snow went from a few inches deep to now nearly touching her ankles over her hiking boots.

Hopefully when the trio had made it to this

point in the trail, Lily was no longer being forced to hike without her shoes. She could imagine Lily now; she'd never been one for long walks, and especially not any that involved her being scared and uncomfortable. Lily had to have been crying the moment she had left the house, and by this point she was probably exhausted and in an overwhelmed flurry of hiccups and sobs.

Elle's chest ached as she thought of Lily and how scared she must have been.

Lily, baby girl, it's going to be okay. She sent up a silent prayer to the universe. Hopefully Lily knew that she was going to come out here looking for her, that she would never let her get hurt… And yet, hadn't she done just that?

She tried to swallow back the guilt that welled in her throat. Guilt would do nothing to make things better; all it would do was obscure her focus on the goal of getting Lily back and into safety.

Daisy pulled harder as they moved up a switchback.

The world was almost pitch-black, and between the falling snow and the enveloping timber, she couldn't even make out light from the stars. Luckily, the city lights from below were reflecting off the clouds and giving her just enough illumination to find her next step.

Lily would have hated this. She hated the dark. On the rare occasions she had been there to put Lily to bed, Lily had always asked for a night-light and for Elle to promise to stand in her room until she had fallen asleep. The first night had taken two hours, three bedtime stories and nearly one million glasses of water and trips to the restroom.

She smiled at the memory and how it brought with it the faint scent of baby powder and new dolls.

Lily would be okay. She had to be okay. *I'm coming for you, baby.*

She sped up.

Maybe the trio had stopped for the night. If they were out here on their own volition, they would have likely called it a night and put down a place for a camp—along with a fire to keep them warm. If they were kidnapped, if the perpetrator wanted to keep them alive and relatively unscathed, he would have needed to let them rest soon.

Which meant all they had to do to catch up with the trio was keep pushing forward.

The wind pressed against her cheeks, blowing down hard from the top of the mountain. Elle pulled in a long breath, hoping to catch the tarry scent of burning pine and a campfire, but she couldn't smell anything but the biting scent of ice.

Without a fire it was unlikely that anyone could survive a night out here, not at the mercy of the elements. Without shoes and drained from miles of hiking, Lily would be especially at risk. She didn't have the body mass or the gear to be out here like she was for any extended period of time, let alone the night hours when the temperature was expected to drop at least another twenty degrees.

Daisy paused.

"What is it, Daisy? *Poshli.*" She took a step, urging the dog forward.

Instead, Daisy sat down and looked up the mountain, signaling.

"What did you find, girl?" She walked to Daisy and searched the ground; she couldn't see anything, and she was forced to flip on the light on her cell phone to illuminate the ground. There, barely poking up from the snow, was a purple mitten.

Lily's mitten.

The lump returned to her throat. Not only did Lily not have shoes, but now she was missing a glove.

Why hadn't they stopped to pick up her glove?

They must have been moving fast. Catherine wasn't the best mother Elle had ever seen, but she was hardly the worst. She had seen terrorists use children in ways that she would have never thought of or expected, but Catherine wasn't the type who would just let her daughter freeze. Catherine loved her.

Elle had to assume she would fight for her daughter. Perhaps that was where the blood they had found had come from. Perhaps it was Catherine's. If she had been in the mother's shoes, she would have fought tooth and nail until they were safe.

Then again, from the trail they had followed so far, there hadn't been any more areas where it looked as though there had been an altercation—at least not when they could make out the tracks in the snow. Did that mean that Catherine had just gone along with the man? Had she allowed herself to be pliable? Or had the man been threatening them? Or was Catherine out here for some purpose that they didn't yet understand?

Grant stopped beside her, taking pictures with his cell phone and noting the mitten for the camera.

The wind washed through the timber, making the branches rub against each other and creating an eerie melody from nature's cello. The sound made chills run down her spine.

It's nothing. I can't be afraid. There's no time for fear. Not for myself.

Clearly, she had watched too many horror flicks, but she couldn't let them seep into this search.

Grant slipped on a pair of nitrile gloves and took out a plastic bag from his pocket. Ever so meticulously, he leaned down and picked up the mitten and glided it into the bag, careful to keep it as pristine as he could, no doubt in an effort to protect any evidence they acquired should they need to take this to court or be judged for their actions later.

They both stared at the glove for a long moment. There was a faint red stain on the seam near the fingertips of the mitten, almost as if Lily had touched a wound with the edge of her glove.

"Does it seem odd to you that they would have remembered to bring her gloves but not boots?" Grant asked.

"If I know anything from my experience with kids, it's that they can never find their shoes when you're in a hurry." There was a wisp of a smile at the corners of her lips, but it was overtaken by the gravity of the moment.

She pointed the light of her phone up the mountain. It was hard to tell how far they were from the peak, or how much farther they would go from here. How far could Lily have gone if she was bloodied and cold?

Not much farther.

"I bet that blood isn't from her. It's probably Catherine's," she said, her voice sounding hollow and dampened by the snowy world around them.

Grant frowned, shrugging. He turned on the light of his phone and illuminated the bagged glove as if doing so would give him the answers they were seeking. "It's possible. But hell, anything is." He clamped his mouth shut like he was refusing to say another damned word on the subject, always the cop. There was nothing they were better at than being unflappable.

She both loved and hated that calm in the face of chaos. Why couldn't he just say what he thought, what he feared? Then again, she had enough fears and imagined outcomes; if he laid his upon her, she wasn't sure she was strong enough to bear the weight.

Why couldn't she be stronger?

Hopefully Lily was proving to be far more formidable. Lily's smiling face floated to the front of her mind, making tears well in her eyes.

The wind rustled through the pines, hard and faster, and there was the drop of snow from branches, the sound reminiscent of footfalls.

Just like the answers, even the forest was attempting to run away from them.

There was a thud and a crack of a branch, and she shined her light in the direction of the sound. She wasn't entirely sure whether or not it was more snow falling or something else, maybe an animal. This time of year, bears were in hibernation, but it could've been something large like an elk or even possibly a mountain lion.

Wouldn't that be crazy, them coming up the mountain looking for the missing Clarks and their possible kidnapper and then she and Grant falling victim to another kind of predator? The darkness in her heart made her laugh at the sick humor.

She looked at Daisy, but the dog was sniffing the ground around where they'd found the mitten and seemed oblivious to the noise coming from the woods. Daisy was good, but just like her, the dog had a habit of being almost myopic when it came to the task at hand.

She moved the beam of her light right to left, and as she was about to look away, she made out the unmistakable glow of two eyes from her peripheral vision. Instinctively, she stepped closer to Daisy and in front of Grant as though she was his shield. She moved the light in the direction of the eyes, but as she did, they disappeared into the thick stand of timber. Though she searched the area where she thought the animal had gone, she didn't see it again.

Daisy wasn't the only animal who seemed to be drawn to Lily—or rather, the scent of blood.

If the scavengers were starting to descend, she and Grant were likely walking into something far more sinister than simply two missing people.

Her stomach roiled at the thought.

She looked to the place where they had found the glove and then up at Grant. She thought about telling him of the eyes in the darkness, but she held back. There were plenty of things to be frightened of, but eyes staring out of the darkness seemed like the most innocuous of the dangers they faced. Whatever animal had been staring at them had been skittish. It was likely more curious than anything else.

Like people, there were different kinds of predators—those who preyed upon weakness and were opportunistic killers, almost scavengers in their selection of their weak quarry, and then there were those predators who sought more challenging prey in order to test their killing abilities. The animal in the woods was likely more the scavenger type and less the stalker... Or perhaps it was situationally dependent. Perhaps the predator in the woods was seeking an easy meal because of the spent blood and wouldn't waste its energy stalking them.

"You okay?" Grant asked. He put his hand on the side of her waist, and the action was so unexpected that she allowed his hand to remain.

She didn't like to be touched.

"Yeah, just thought I saw something, but it was nothing." It was strange how she wanted to protect this man. Instead of stepping away, she wanted to reach out, to shield him.

Or maybe it wasn't about the man at all. Maybe she was just acting this way in an effort to protect herself from feeling more fear. But now wasn't the time for some deep introspection; no, this was the time for Lily.

He motioned up the hill. "Do you see that up there?"

She had no idea what he was talking about. "What?"

He pointed his finger more vehemently as if his simple action would clarify the entire situation for her. "Up there, see that line in the snow? There, under the tree." He shined the beam of his flashlight near the base of a large fir tree.

She finally spotted what appeared to be a drag mark in the snow. Though they were at least a dozen yards from the spot, it appeared to be the approximate width of a body.

Carefully, they picked their way straight up

the hillside, moving through deadfall. There was the snap of sticks and the crunch of the snow as they slowly struggled upward. It was steep, and as they neared the tree, Grant grunted. She glanced in his direction in time to watch him slip, then catch and right himself.

If that mark in the snow was a drag mark, how could anyone move a body through this? They could barely walk through it on their own even without a three-year-old.

When she was growing up, her father had taught her to hunt. When he wasn't jetting around the world and taking down bad guys for the US government, he had taken her and her siblings out into the woods. They had spent time every fall and early winter in the woods, tracking and learning the patterns of animals. Her father had always told her it was so they could be more in touch with nature, but as she grew older, she realized it was just as much about human nature as it was about flora and fauna.

One of the things that her father had drilled into her was that when animals and humans were injured, they would look for areas of cover. Most animals would run downhill toward water sources—creek beds and rivers. If water wasn't close by or if they were significantly injured, they would seek shelter from trees.

As she stopped to catch her breath, she realized that what they were looking at wasn't likely to be a drag mark from someone being pulled up the hill, but it was more likely whoever had been hiding had slid down. They were, simply put, injured prey hiding from the predator. Little had they known, but predators and scavengers were everywhere around them.

Daisy whined, pulling hard at the lead and nosing in the direction of the tree.

"I know, Daisy." She tried to control her heavy breathing; until now she hadn't realized how much the hike had taken out of her. "Hello?" she called, hoping that if there was someone at the base of the tree, someone they couldn't yet see, that they would call out an answer…anything, even a grunt that could act as a sign of life.

Grant was a few steps ahead of her and stopped as she called out, but there was nothing, only the cascading sounds of the winter wind. Somehow, the world around them felt colder.

Ascending the last few yards, in the thin light she could make out the edge of a bench beneath the tree, a flattened area that sometimes naturally occurred under large, aged trees thanks to years of deadfall accumulation, which then became alcoves.

She silently prayed she was wrong, that her years of wilderness training were making her jump to the wrong conclusions. For all she knew, the animal they had run into below had made a kill and was actually watching them to make sure they didn't find its quarry.

Goose bumps rose on her skin.

It was strange how a person's sixth sense could pique and the mind could usher it away with a million different reasons to not pay it heed. Yet, when it came down to the critical moment, it was usually the sixth sense that would be proven right.

Daisy leaped up and over the edge of the bench and immediately sat down, indicating something. Grant stood beside her, holding out his hand and helping Elle up the last step so she could be beside the dog.

The bench under the tree was larger than she had thought it would have been—it was approximately as wide as the widest point of the tree's canopy, and as she stepped up, the dead limbs of the tree tore at her hair and scraped against her cheeks, forcing her to push the limbs away. It was really no wonder animals would have chosen this alcove to tuck in and away from the world.

Grant grunted as he stepped up. She held back the branches so he could move beside her without being ripped to shreds by the gnarled fingers of the protective sentry. The dry twig in her hand snapped, the sound making her jump.

"You're okay," Grant whispered, as though he was just as at odds with the fear in his gut as she was. His hand found its way to her waist again, and this time instead of merely allowing his touch, she moved into it ever so slightly.

"I'm fine," she lied.

He moved the beam of his flashlight in the direction of the base of the tree, but there were so many branches that he was forced to crouch down. As he moved, he sucked in a breath.

She dropped to her knees in the snow and dirt beside him. There, slumped against the gray bark, was a woman. Her hands were palm up in her lap. She listed to the right, and her face and shoulder were pressed into the brackish moss and bark. Her face was down, but thanks to the bottled, platinum-blond color of her hair, Elle knew she was staring at Catherine.

She glanced at Catherine's fingers. The tips were purple, but her skin was the gray-white that only came with death.

Chapter Six

The Two Bear helo touched down at the top of the mountain just short of midnight on one of the longest days of Grant's life. He had thought he had been in good shape, but apparently a six-plus-mile hike straight up the face of a mountain wasn't something his body was adequately prepared for. He waited as the coroner stepped out of the helicopter, followed by a few more members of the search and rescue team.

The members of the team who had come up from the bottom of the mountain had finally caught up with them, and those volunteers were now in a holding pattern, sitting and resting while they waited for the helo team.

The commander, Melody, stepped out and made her way toward him, holding her head and crouching down to protect herself from the rotor's wash. "Any new information?" she called over the noise of the blades.

He shook his head and motioned for her to

follow him toward the rest of their waiting team. The helicopter took off, dipping its nose as it turned and descended back down toward the valley and the city at its heart.

Part of him wished he was on the bird, having completed the task and having found Lily and the man who was still at large. Unfortunately, he had fallen short.

The coroner followed in Melody's wake, looking down at his phone like he was deep into reading something on the screen. As they stopped, the coroner bumped into her. "Whoa, sorry," he said, finally looking up. "How long has it been since you found the deceased?"

Well, at least he wasn't one for screwing around.

"It's been about two hours."

"And you said she was limp when you found her? No signs of rigor mortis setting in?" The coroner made a note on his phone.

"We only touched her to try and get a pulse, but her neck was soft to the touch."

The coroner nodded. He was all about getting straight to the point. If only Grant had more people in his life who ran on that kind of a timeline. Elle was just starting a campfire as he glanced over at her. As if feeling his gaze, she looked at him. Their eyes connected for a moment, and he could see that hers were red and tired.

She needed to get off this mountain, or at the very least take a rest and then start fresh in the morning. Yet he was sure that no matter what he said to her, or how hard he tried to convince her, there was nothing he could do to pull her away from this. She wasn't going to stop until Lily was safe.

Unfortunately, their trail had run dry. No matter how much Daisy had sniffed and searched, it seemed as if where Catherine's body had been found was also the last place there had been any active scent. They had spent at least an hour while they had waited for the teams, looking for any leads. Nothing. It was almost as if Lily and the presumed man had disappeared the moment Catherine died.

As the flames took hold and enveloped the logs in the fire, Elle made her way over to them. Melody and the SAR team who had just arrived sat down next to the four already around the fire, and they all started talking, something about maps and directions. A few were checking their radios and getting ready for the dog and pony show.

The coroner looked up from his notes. "From the temperature out here currently and from what information you have given me, I think it is fair to assume that our victim has been dead for no more than four to six hours based on the primary indicators. The cold has kept her from going into full rigor mortis, but I would expect, given her glycogen output hiking up the hill, if my math is correct, the victim will probably start having the onset of rigor mortis within the next hour. But first I must see the vic."

He wasn't sure what to make of the information. Did that mean that the coroner wanted to get her off the mountain before she was completely immobilized?

"Can you take me to her?" the coroner asked, holding on to the strap of the satchel that was crossed over his chest.

Elle looked at him, asking for an invitation though she said nothing aloud. "Yeah," Grant said, "Elle, why don't you join us?"

She gave him a tip of the head in thanks, but the coroner gave her a quick side-eye before sighing and shrugging her presence off.

"Let's go," the coroner said, pointing vaguely downhill. "It is colder than the backside of the moon up here, and I have a hot cup of coffee with my name on it sitting in my living room."

Was that the sand in this man's craw? That he was having to come out to the woods in the cold in the middle of the night in order to retrieve a body?

He had met the deputy coroner a few times—he worked in the same office, but the deputy coroner was on the other side and they rarely shared more than a few words socially. Now, he wasn't too upset that his time had been limited with the officer. They were definitely cut from different cloth. When he'd been acting as coroner a few years ago, he was always jonesing to go on a call—not that he wished anyone an ill fate—he just found the work fascinating. It was a small thing, helping the dead find rest. Yet it brought solace to the victims' families, and someone had to do it.

If Grant hadn't become a cop, he wouldn't have minded going to work as a medical examiner. He always loved working through a good mystery, and nothing was more confusing than people—though the living were far more confusing than the dead.

Elle led the way down the hill, taking the broken trail until they were standing just above the ledge and the tree where Catherine could be found.

The coroner looked over his shoulder at him, like he found it a nuisance that he was going to have to crawl down over the ledge and onto the bench to get to the deceased woman. Yep, this coroner would need some more hours on this job. It was a great learning opportunity, but it seemed as though the kid was not quite realizing that just yet. Until he did, Grant would make sure to make a few calls when he got back to the office.

Grant and Elle climbed down onto the bench, carefully working around the limbs of the tree until they once again found themselves face-to-face—well, rather face to *head*—with Catherine. The coroner took a series of photographs, making sure that they were holding up lights to help illuminate the scene.

The coroner clicked his tongue a few times before reaching into his satchel and taking out a pair of nitrile gloves. He set to work taking more pictures and then going over the body. He took measurements of the scene, documenting everything in his phone before finally touching Catherine's head. He moved her chin up and peered under her neck. There, beneath the base of her chin, was a large abrasion. "Hmm."

He took another picture and made a note.

The coroner's movements were slow, methodical as he started at the top of the woman's body and worked his way down. He unzipped her jacket. Her white silk blouse was stained deep crimson red, some areas so dark that it was almost black with blood. At the center of the blackness were slits in the cloth and the flesh beneath.

Grant sucked in a breath.

"Yep," the coroner said, sounding unsurprised, "looks like we have found the most likely cause of death. Looks like we have at least ten or fifteen puncture wounds here, but the medical examiner will have to open her up for the official count—and the weapon used, but from what I can see… I'd guess it was a large fixed-blade knife. There are some wide, deep punctures here." He moved back a bit of the woman's stained shirt to expose what looked like a two-inch-long stab wound.

As he moved the shirt slightly, Elle let out a thin wheezing sound, making Grant turn.

Tears were streaming down her face, and Daisy was licking her hand. He hadn't been thinking. If he had been, he would have never put her in the position to watch her former employer being poked and prodded.

He wrapped his arm around her shoulder and led her away. Whatever the coroner found, he could tell them later. For now, Grant needed get her the hell out of there.

Elle's body was rigid under his arm, but she didn't resist as he led her away. Daisy followed in their footsteps, watching warily as her mistress slowly picked her way back up the hill. It took twenty minutes to climb to the top of the mountain, where the SAR team had moved out, leaving the campfire gently flickering in the darkness. To the north, he could make out the thin lights of their flashlights as they started to make their way over to the other side of the mountain saddle.

As he stood with Elle in the thin firelight, watching the beams of flashlights bounce around and move between the smattering of trees at the top of the mountain, he couldn't help but feel the futility in their situation. If their kidnapper was capable of such a brutal murder, one with possibly dozens of stab wounds, they had to be angry. And when a killer was so filled with rage, there was no telling what they might do—and not even a child would be considered out of bounds when it came to murder.

Chapter Seven

Elle didn't know when she fell asleep—she sure as hell hadn't meant to, not with everything happening. Yet, at some point when she had been sitting beside the fire wrapped in Grant's warm embrace with Daisy on her feet, she must have succumbed to her exhaustion. As she woke, she looked out at the fire. During the night, someone must have kept it fed, as it was in full roar, a trio of large blackened logs at its heart.

She was lying on a bed of pine boughs, and there was a thin Mylar blanket over her. It surprised her that she had been sleeping so hard that someone could have moved her in such a way, but at the same time, exhaustion had that effect on her. Honestly, she couldn't recall a time she had been more physically or emotionally drained.

She had been in some real pits of hell before—her thoughts drifted back to the empty pair of shoes at the bomb site—but even then, she had struggled to find sleep. During that time in her life, she had turned to sleeping pills and vodka. Her body never allowed her to sleep like she had last night.

There was the crunch of footsteps in the snow behind her, and she considered pretending she was still asleep. Yet, no matter how much she wanted to hide from the reality that she was confronted with, Lily depended on her.

She turned. Grant was standing with his back to her, looking out at the sun as it peeked over the top of the mountains to the east. Daisy was seated on the ground beside him, and he was scratching behind her ears. Of course, Daisy would be amenable to a good-looking man who wanted to give her attention. And yet, Elle couldn't help but be a little bit jealous that the dog had given herself so freely over to the man.

"Where is everyone?" she asked, sitting up.

"After you fell asleep, I helped the coroner bag Catherine's remains. Two Bear dropped the line from the helo, and we got her on board." He took out his phone and peered down at the screen. "Catherine's remains were transported to the medical examiner's office, where they are already performing an autopsy. They found hair samples on her body, and they have started performing DNA analysis in hope we can find the identity of the murderer."

She nodded, wishing she was slightly more awake so she could make sense of everything that Grant was trying to tell her without the fuzziness of having just woken. "I'm sorry I fell asleep. You should've woken me. I could've been out there helping you guys." She was suddenly embarrassed that he had witnessed her inability to keep pace with what the situation required. "Where's the SAR team? Have they found anything, any idea as to Lily's location? Has there been a ransom call?"

He looked down at his hands as he scratched Daisy's head slightly more vigorously. "No calls. Yet. They have started working their way down the mountain. This morning, actually about an hour ago, on the other side of the mountain saddle, they found evidence that a helicopter had been on-site."

"Another helicopter, as in one besides Two Bear?" She was confused.

"When Two Bear airlifted the SAR team out, we talked to them, and they said they hadn't been in that specific area—we are thinking someone picked up Lily and her kidnapper before you and I made it to Catherine."

"How do they know it was Lily?" She heard the frantic note in her voice.

"They found a child's tracks near the pickup site. They were covered by last night's snowfall. Lily is gone, airlifted out. If nothing else, at least we know she is still alive and didn't have to spend the night on the mountain."

Thank goodness. "Is there any way we can track her helicopter? There has to be some kind of flight record, right?"

"I have my teams working on that, but whoever this kidnapper is, they have resources that up until now we weren't aware of."

She put her hands over her face and rubbed at her temples. "We were so close. We had a chance to save her…"

He put his hands up in surrender. "It's okay, we will find her. She's relatively unharmed. She's going to be okay."

"You can't tell me any of that." She stood up, the motion so fast that her head swam. She reached out, but there was nothing to support her and Grant rushed to her side. "I don't believe you." She tried to pull away from his touch, but her body was unsteady and he gripped her harder to keep her from falling.

"You need to sit down for a minute. You're probably really dehydrated after yesterday. Did you even drink any water?" He reached behind him and grabbed a water bottle that had been clipped to his utility belt. He opened up the lid with a squeak and handed it over.

Though she was upset, she allowed him to

help her to sit and took the water. She hadn't realized how thirsty she was until the ice-cold liquid hit her parched lips. She closed the bottle and handed it back to him with a nod. Logically she knew she wasn't angry with the man who was trying his very best to help her, yet all she wanted to do was snarl and bite at him. Why did he have to be so perfect, having everything she needed before she even knew she needed it—all while looking sexy?

She took another swig of water and reached up to touch her hair, forgetting she was wearing a knit cap. Her hair poked out from under the edge of the hat above her ears, and she could instantly envision what a mess she must have looked like. Running her fingers over her cheek, she could feel the indentations made by the pine boughs; there was even a small pine needle stuck to the side of her cheek, and she had to scratch to free it from her skin.

Though, what did it really matter what she looked like right now?

The fact she cared about that at all concerned her more than her actual appearance. She wasn't one to get too wrapped up in vanity, but when she was, under these circumstances, it made her wonder what she wasn't admitting to herself when it came to her feelings toward Grant.

His hand was on her shoulder, and she found herself enjoying the warmth of his touch.

He barely knew her, and he had gone out of his way last night to make sure that she was comfortable and warm. Taking care of her in her moment of greatest weakness. Did that mean that he also felt something, or did it just fall under the scope of him being the nearly picture-perfect hero he seemed to be?

No. She almost shook her head. *If he is perfect, we would have Lily back in our custody. She would have never had the time to get away.*

As quickly as the angry thoughts came to her, she batted them away. It wasn't Grant's fault she had allowed the little girl to fall into the wrong hands. This was all her fault…everything could be pinned down to her and her error in judgments.

"What's the matter? Are you okay? Do you need anything?" Grant asked, sitting down on the ground beside her.

Daisy trotted over and gave her a quick lick to the face as if she, too, could tell that Elle was struggling. She wrapped her arm around the dog's neck, and Daisy perched against her, nuzzling her snout under Elle's chin and snuggling in as she hugged her. "I love you, angel," she whispered into the dog's fur.

There was nothing like a dog's touch to calm

the most turbulent storms in the soul. Hopefully Lily had an animal with her, something that she could touch that would help her stay calm—that was, if she was still alive.

A sob threatened to escape from her throat, but she tried to bite it back. She was too slow, and the sound rattled from her, far too loud.

Grant's hand moved to her knee, and he put his other arm around her, surrounding her with his stupidly perfect body. Didn't he realize that he was making this all so much worse by being kind? If he would just stop helping her, she could control some of the weakness and stonewall it with her normal aplomb and resolve. What was it about this man that made her break down and actually *feel*?

His thumb gently stroked her inner thigh, and she felt what little control she still had drift from her. Didn't he realize what he was doing to her? He was going to make her totally melt down. There would be tears. No woman in the world wanted to wake up and just go straight to fear and crying over the things that were outside her control.

There was only one way she was going to get out of this moment by not breaking down and just crying in front of him again. She had to do it if she wanted to save what little pride she had left.

Before she had a chance to reconsider her impulsive thought, she leaned over and pushed her lips to his. He hadn't been ready, but neither was she, and his lips were pulled into a thin smile, making it so she kissed the cool slickness of his teeth.

What was I thinking? Gah, I can be so stupid sometimes.

Embarrassment filled her and she started to move, but before she could pull away, he took her face in his hands and closed his mouth and kissed her back. The tip of his tongue darted out, and he moved it gently against her bottom lip; she followed, tasting the lingering sweetness of his gum and the bite of the cold mountain air. He caressed her cheeks with his thumbs, and his lips slowed, moving her starved, hurried action into a sultry, deep kiss. It was like he could read her mind, follow her thoughts… thoughts and desires she didn't even know she had…and yet that he could satisfy.

If she hadn't gone through so many emotions, she would have called this her very best first kiss. What if this was her last first kiss?

What if she had screwed up her best first kiss by stealing it in the wrong moment but with the right man?

Worse, what if she had just had her first and last kiss with Grant? What if he was once again just trying to save her feelings by doing what he thought she wanted him to do and once they got back down into the valley and back to their lives, he would let her down gracefully? What if none of this was real? Or what if he was only kissing her because she was kissing him—was it just some kiss of opportunity?

As his tongue flicked against hers, she tried to force herself back in the moment, to stop thinking about all the things that were flipping through her mind. Daisy plopped down on her foot and let out a long sigh. The sound made her smile, and as she did, Grant let his hands move from her face and he sat back.

"Was my kiss that bad?"

"What?" she asked, finally opening her eyes and looking at him. "No…that's not it." He had the best eyes—they were green around the outsides and brown in the middle, and in the thin morning light they even picked up bits of gray and purple from the sky.

His eyes, just like the man to which they belonged, were perfect. They were everything, every color…he was the embodiment of all the things she wanted to see and feel, and damn it if he didn't make every part of her body spark with want. But she couldn't have him.

She stood up, carefully away from Daisy, and Grant moved to reach for her, but she noted how he stopped himself. Maybe he realized they were wrong, too. Maybe he had seen her kiss for what she had intended it to be—a stopgap in the moment, anything to make her stop feeling. And then…well, and then it screwed everything up.

She turned her back to him, afraid if she looked into that perfect face and those perfect eyes she would sink back down to the ground and beg for him to take her into his arms. Closing her eyes, she reached up and touched the place on her lip where his tongue had brushed against her. It was still wet from their kiss, and she gently licked the residue.

She tasted like him, and she wished she could keep that flavor on her lips forever—it could be the one part of him that she could keep. The rest of him, she had to let go. Not only was she far too big of a dumpster fire to think having a relationship was a good idea, but she needed to get Lily back and make sure that she would still have a job with STEALTH after this major screwup.

"Elle, you don't need to run away from me."

Oh yes, she did. But unless she and Daisy were about to jog down a damned mountain by themselves, there weren't a whole lot of places she could run to.

"I'm not running away." *Not a lie.* "I just…"

Can't get caught up in falling for someone right now, or ever. "I don't want to…"

"It's okay," he said, sounding dejected. "You don't need to tell me that you think it was a mistake to kiss me. You're hardly the first woman to kiss and run."

Now that sounded like a story from his past that she wanted to hear, but if she stopped and asked him about it, he might get the wrong idea.

"What is wrong with women?" he countered.

Every hair on the back of her neck stood up. "What in the hell is that supposed to mean?"

His face fell, and he gave her an apologetic stare; he looked like Lily did when she knew she had said something she wasn't supposed to and had been overheard. Unlike Lily, she couldn't send Grant to the corner for a timeout and a moment to reflect on his mistake.

"I… I don't mean you… I just meant…"

"You most certainly did mean me," she seethed. "Have you men ever stopped to think that maybe it isn't the women who *have something wrong* with them? Have you ever considered that maybe it's men and their failure to actually talk to women? Maybe if you could actually take a moment and express yourself carefully and with accurate language, maybe we could work together?"

"Whoa," he said, sitting back like she had just thrown mud at him. "I… I'm sorry."

She turned to the fire and kicked a pile of snow atop the flames; the logs sizzled as the ice hit them and instantly evaporated into the dry air. She kicked again and again as Grant tried to talk to her, but she blocked him out with the manic kicking and her heaving breaths as she fought the fire, choking it out.

As she worked herself down off the edge of anger, she realized her mistake. Grant hadn't meant to be misogynistic, not the now not-quite-as-perfect specimen of man. He had definitely misspoken, but he wasn't guilty of the things that she had called him out for being.

Just like his statement about kissing and running, it was easy to tell that her own baggage had come back to be hauled out and strewn into the open.

"Elle," he whispered her name, begging, "please listen to me."

Exhausted by her fury, she took a deep breath and released it into the steam rising from the fire. Finally, she turned but said nothing as she looked at him. She didn't know what she wanted him to say to her, or what she should say to him. If anything, she should have apologized for her outburst. She was embarrassed by her overreaction, but at the same time, she had found something cathartic in the meltdown. Maybe Lily and her toddler tantrums had worn off on her, but if they had, there was something to be said for their efficacy in bringing her back to an internal stasis.

She dropped her hands to her sides, releasing the tension from her shoulders as she finally met his pleading gaze. "I'm listening," she said plaintively.

He reached up and took her hands in his, squeezing them. "I think you are so beautiful. I kissed you because I wanted to kiss you. And damn it, if you'd let me, I'd kiss you again—"

"But," she said, interrupting. It was only what he said after the *but* that would really matter. Those words would be the ones he truly meant, the ones that weren't said to assuage the pain but instead would do the tearing.

"*But* you aren't in a good place right now."

She opened her mouth to speak, or perhaps it was from the shock of his words. Did he mean that she was too big of a mess to give love to? Or did he mean that he thought she would never be in a place where they could be together?

Well, if he felt even remotely close to either of those things, she didn't need him. Her anger threatened to boil back up thanks to the salt he had thrown.

She closed her mouth. Maybe he wasn't wrong;

she had already admitted to herself that she was a dumpster fire right now. But how dare he actually call her out for it?

Could she really be upset with him for saying what she had clearly been unable to hide?

No. She couldn't be. It wasn't his fault for the way she was feeling. It was only hers.

All she could really do was try to find the stasis she had thought she had brought into her life only moments before. It sucked, feeling this unbalanced. If only there was some simple fix—if only his kiss could have been that for her.

Though it had led to nothing more than a few extra hurt feelings, at least she had tried. For a moment, he had given her an escape from her thoughts, but it was her responsibility to set things right.

She squeezed his hands as she closed her eyes, taking in the smell of the campfire and the world around them.

He was a sweet man. He was trying to do the right thing. No matter how badly she wanted to push him away and tell him he was wrong in his assessment of her, she couldn't deny the nearly perfect man hadn't missed the mark.

He stood up and let go of her hands so he could wrap his arms around her. He pulled her into his embrace and held her there. She went rigid for a moment, at odds with all the feelings and thoughts inside her, but as his breath caressed her cheek and warmed her, she fell into the rhythm of him. She wished he wasn't wearing a heavy coat so she could hear his heart. It was strange how listening to another person's heartbeat could bring calm. More than calm—she couldn't help but wonder if that in this instance listening to his heartbeat would also bring some semblance of love.

She needed to press herself away at the mere consideration or fluttering of the word *love* from within her. That was the real fire. That word, that sensation, had the power to burn down everything, including the feeble foundation of self-control she was teetering upon.

"You're okay." He whispered the words into her hair, but as he spoke, she could hear the thumping of a helicopter moving toward them in the distance.

As relieved as she was to hear the chopper coming, she couldn't help feeling disappointment, as well. She needed this moment, one only his embrace could provide.

Chapter Eight

His father had always told him that the key to a good life was to live for today and prepare for tomorrow. It had been two days since he had spoken to Elle, and he couldn't help the feeling that if he had heeded his father's advice, his life could have been going in an entirely different direction. If only he had given in to more than just her kiss, if only he had told her that he wanted her…all of her.

Sure, they didn't need to act on it, but if he had just told her all the things that had been roiling inside him at least she could have known, and he could have been free from going over the what-ifs.

He'd had no excuse to contact her, which made it worse. The case wasn't moving, and the trail seemed cold. No ransom calls had come in. No new information. He knew there were others in DC working it—with a US senator involved, FBI and Secret Service were in the mix—but they weren't sharing information in anything approaching a fulsome way. No one on his team had even been able to get to the senator for an interview. Two days after his wife's murder and daughter's disappearance.

Luckily, it was only in his downtime, the hours after he came home and was standing in the shower, that his mind had been allowed to wander to that night spent on the mountain beside Elle. She had been so sexy, lying there in the campfire light, the oranges and reds picking up the bits of copper in her dark locks and making them shimmer in the night.

He couldn't think of any other woman who'd stayed in his mind that way, where he remembered those kinds of details about her. It made him almost feel bad. He had been with his ex-girlfriend for two years. He had loved her, but he could barely even remember the feel of her hair in his fingers or the color of it in the moonlight. Yet he had spent one night with Elle—probably one of the hardest nights she had ever experienced—and he couldn't get the thoughts of her out of his mind.

Had he really ever loved his ex like he had thought he had? Or were time and absence making those little details, the ones he was noticing about Elle, disappear from his memory? He hoped it was time, because every woman he professed to love deserved to be loved with as much energy and feeling as he could muster. What was love if not given in its entirety?

Any man worth his weight should give his woman every ounce of himself. It was why he couldn't understand cheating. While he could understand the ability to love more than one person in life, he couldn't understand how a person could have enough love to give two people everything they had at the same time. It was impossible. And if a person wasn't giving all of their love to the person they were with, and had the capacity to spill the same romantic love out to others, then they had to have been with the wrong person.

That was what had happened with his ex. He hadn't cheated, but he found that he could suddenly look at other women and think about wanting them. In that moment, he had known his relationship with her was over. She was a good woman, a lawyer, but he couldn't be with anyone whom he couldn't give himself fully to. She deserved better, a love that would keep them both up at night. And he loved her enough to give that to her, even if that meant it was another man who gave her all she deserved.

It had hurt to let her go, even more when he explained that he didn't think he was enough for her, and she hadn't wanted to accept his rationale. Yet, in the end they had gone their separate ways as friends. She had married a doctor a year later, and Grant couldn't have been happier for her.

Sometimes, like now, he found he was jealous of her ability to move on and find the right man for her while he was still single, but he was happy for her. She deserved the best things in life, and if life wasn't ready to bring him the same grace of happiness…well, he had to just accept the things it did have to offer.

As he turned off the shower and stepped out and started drying off, his thoughts moved back to Elle. Was she the one he was supposed to have in his life? Was that why every thought he had came back to her? Or was it that he was addicted to her because in that moment on the hillside he got to be her knight in shining armor?

He nearly groaned at the thought. He did not just think that.

Yep. There had to be something wrong with him. Maybe he needed to just have a few more minutes alone in the shower in order to clear his mind. Yeah, that could have been it.

She wasn't interested in him. If she had been, she would have called him by now. As it was, he was surprised she hadn't called him to check in on the case. Two days was a hell of a long time when there was a little girl missing.

So far, they had managed to track down the helicopter that had picked up the man and Lily. It had come from the Neptune airfield and was owned by a private party who was hard to track. It was registered to an LLC out of Nevada called NightGens, and when he had tried to call the company it was registered to, he had only come to voice mails and dead ends. Even their address was just some lawyer's office in Las Vegas, and that fellow had been close-mouthed, not even willing to admit he handled the business. Grant had reached out to LVPD, and they'd done him a solid by scoping out the airfield only to come up empty. It had looked abandoned.

Whoever owned that helicopter must have loved their anonymity, or else the person who had hired them had known they needed a company and a team that could keep them from being found. Either way, it made his investigation and search for the little girl that much harder.

Luckily, Deputy Terrill had taken the lead on Lily's disappearance and had been putting boots on the ground when Grant was off shift. His phone had been pinging nonstop with updates from the teams, but so far everyone had been coming up empty-handed.

The little girl's father, Dean Clark, was set to return to the state today, and Grant would be at the airport waiting to pick him up the minute his plane touched down. The senator had been informed of his wife's death and his daughter's disappearance but had been playing on the stage in Washington, DC, and some office assistant had informed him Senator Clark was working with federal authorities and would talk to him when he returned.

Grant had a hard time not being angry with the man. In this day and age, when information availability was nearly immediate, he couldn't believe that the senator hadn't bothered to check in with the law enforcement who'd first been on the scene. Then, there was nothing about this case that hadn't been a goat rope. If things started to go smoothly and things just easily clicked into place, Grant wasn't sure if he would have trusted it.

From what Grant had been told, the senator hadn't received the news well, which was to be expected. One of the members of the team who had been tasked with tracking him down had managed to talk to the agent who'd first given Clark the news. The senator had actually begun to cry. It was the man's one saving grace in being nearly inaccessible.

In an investigation with a wife and child involved, normally the first suspect on any list for a disappearance or death was the spouse. They were usually the ones with the motive and opportunity. However, from the limited number of interviews they had been doing with household staff and neighbors, including the one who had reported the crime, the senator and his wife appeared to be the picture-perfect couple.

He had even been able to pull the phone records for both Catherine and Dean, and neither had seemed to have any dastardly texts or phone calls from lovers. Really, on paper, they were just as picturesque as everyone had touted them to be. Then again, Elle had made a point of telling him how everything would be exactly that way with this family.

No one on his teams had yet to figure out who the other people had been in the house the day of the kidnapping, the ones Elle had seen. They'd reached out to neighbors, friends, business associates. And fingerprints had been smudged or nonexistent. If those men had been involved, they were smart enough to wipe things down.

After putting on his shoes and grabbing his phone, Grant headed out to his department-issued truck. His phone pinged, and he considered not looking at it while he got settled into his driver's seat.

But it could be Elle. He couldn't gain control of the thought, and if he was honest with himself, it was the only thought he had every time his phone had gone off since he had left her.

She had almost run away from him when they had come down from the mountain. Unfortunately, he had been forced to go in and write up his report about what had happened up there and then give it to the oncoming teams. He had told her to call him and given her his card, but... yeah, nothing.

Maybe she had lost his card. Maybe she'd left it in her pants pocket and then washed it, making it into the little crispy white ball of paper that he so often found when doing his own laundry.

He took out his phone and looked down at the screen. It was another of the deputies who had been on last night. Apparently, they'd had just about as much luck as he and his team had in tracking down any leads.

If they didn't find something soon, anything that could point to Lily's location, he feared that the little girl would get lost to the system. Sure, no one would ever just say they would stop looking, but the everyday grind of what they did, answering calls and serving warrants, had a way of pulling attention away from the crimes that he truly wished he could solve.

If he never found Lily, he would never forgive himself. Elle would never forgive him. From the look on her face when he had told her about Lily going missing from the mountain, he couldn't help but feel like she was already blaming him for not having found her. If only they had hiked faster, if he hadn't slowed them down, maybe they would have made it to Catherine before she had been murdered… And if they hadn't focused so much on Catherine's body, maybe they could have made it to Lily before she had been swept off the mountain.

There had to be answers, something he was missing.

For now, though, he had to call Elle. He had to know she was okay. Hopefully she was doing better than the last time he had seen her. She had been such a mess; her emotions were all over the map and all he could do was be there. It hadn't been enough. Not when all he wanted to do was set things right and be the hero whom she had so desperately needed and yet he had been unable to become.

He had let her down.

He pulled her information up on his computer and found her phone number. Hopefully she wouldn't be too freaked out that he was taking the lead and calling her first. If she was, he would play it off like he was doing his job and nothing more. Hell, he *was* just doing his job by making sure that she was home and well cared for. He could even pull the Daisy card and ask about how the pup was doing; a hike like that could be hard on a dog.

He punched in her number, and after the third ring he was just about to hang up when he heard the distinct click of her picking up the call. "Hello?" she asked. Her voice sounded tired.

Hopefully she had been taking care of herself.

"Hey, Ms. Spade? This is Sergeant Anders from the Missoula County Sheriff's Office. How are you doing today?" What was wrong with him? Why did he go into full professional mode even though all he wanted to do was be himself and ask her all about herself?

It was no wonder she hadn't reached out to him.

"Hello, Sergeant," she said, but she sounded slightly confused. "I'm doing…okay."

He read into the silence of her answer—no doubt she was worried about Lily. How could he have been so stupid as to ask her how she was doing—she wouldn't be all right.

"Did you find her?" she asked, fear flecking her voice.

Of course that would be why she would think he was calling. The pit in his stomach deepened. For once, he wished he could be the hero. "Unfortunately, no. I was calling to check in on you."

There was a prolonged silence, so long that for a moment he wondered if the call had been dropped. He was going to say her name, but then he heard her breath.

"Like I said, I'm okay." She cleared her throat. "But what has happened…it shouldn't matter how I'm feeling. The only thing that matters to me is Lily. If you want me to be okay, I need her to be found and be safe."

He felt like he was on the stand in the courtroom, every action he took or would take being called into question. If he was in her shoes, though, he would be just as adamant about what needed to be done…and if anything, if things weren't being handled as he wanted them to be, he'd be taking matters into his own hands.

Given who her family was, he had to wonder if she was doing the same. Yet he wasn't sure how he could bring it up. She and her crew weren't the normal armchair quarterbacks; they knew what they were doing and had resources that even he and the department didn't have— on top of it all, they didn't have to adhere to the same set of rules and standards that he and his teams did. STEALTH group had lateral freedoms that he envied. It was really no wonder that when it came to international matters, one of the best weapons the government had was military contractors.

From what he knew about their group and others like it, they worked under the UN and had some immunity and leeway others didn't.

"Elle, about your team and your family…" he started.

"What about us?"

"Have you guys made any progress on the case, gotten anything my teams haven't?" He didn't even bother to ask her *if* they were working on this.

She gave a thin chuckle. "I don't know everything your team has pulled, but we have been running into roadblocks. You find the LLC, the one that owns the helo and airport?"

"Is that why you haven't called me? You didn't need me to get answers?" And did she not miss him at all? He tried to make it sound cute, his insecurities, by giving a little laugh, but even to his own ears it sounded false.

She mustn't have been thinking about him like he had been thinking about her. If she had, there wasn't a chance she had gone this long without reaching out. He had waited as long as he humanly could.

"I was actually planning on calling you later today. I was hoping you had gotten farther ahead." There was a tension in her voice that he wanted to assume was her own attraction and pull to him, one that matched his own. "Do you want to meet up today? There are a few things that I wanted to look into, and I was hoping you could give me some of the findings, if there are any, about Catherine's autopsy."

Though he was more than aware he shouldn't have been excited about seeing her and discussing the dead and missing, he couldn't help himself. He would take every second he could get with Elle, even if it wasn't in date form.

"Sure, they are supposed to be wrapping things up and getting the last toxicology findings today. I'll give the medical examiner a call and see if I can pull the full reports. In the meantime, I'm heading to my office. Meet me there."

WHEN HE ARRIVED at the courthouse and headed up the stairs to headquarters, she was already standing outside the nondescript door that led to the back offices. It made him wonder if she had been inside his world before. Most people didn't know anything about his department or their sanctum aside from it being on the third floor. It constantly surprised him how well his world of law enforcement was masked from the public eye just by being hidden in plain sight.

When she saw him walking up the steps, she smiled, and it was so real that it hit her eyes. He loved that smile, the way it lit her up even though their lives were dark and heavy. Did he have the same lightness? With all the things he had witnessed and been a part of—the lives that had ended in his hands and the worlds he had watched collapse—it wouldn't have surprised him if that part of him had died.

"Hi," she said, giving him a small wave.

He swallowed, trying to keep control of the emotions that were working through him. "Hey. No Daisy today?"

She shook her head as he walked by her and keyed in the code to open the office door.

"She is back at the ranch, hanging with the pack."

"The ranch?" he asked.

Elle nodded as he opened the door and motioned for her to walk ahead.

"Yeah, my team stays at the group's headquarters at the Widow Maker. They have quite a spread, and each year it is getting bigger." She slipped by him as she spoke, and he couldn't help but look at how her black, firehouse-cloth pants hugged her curves.

She did have some great curves. From the lines on her ass, she liked bikini-style underwear. Probably red. No. Blue. She seemed like the kind of woman who wanted relaxed, easygoing lovemaking. In his limited experience, it was the women who wore red panties who were the wild things and those who leaned more toward blue who were more of his speed.

He couldn't look away from the way her hips swayed as they made their way down the hall toward his office until she turned around and looked at him. He jerked, hoping she didn't notice him looking at her like he had been. She didn't need to think he was some kind of pervert. He wasn't like many of the other cops, guys who were all about their dicks. Sure, he could pull any number of women, but he didn't want just anyone. He was looking for a whole lot more than just sex.

She said something about the case, bringing his thoughts back to work and he turned away and pretended to read a flyer someone had tacked to the corkboard until he could regain his composure.

"Did you hear me?" she asked, walking back to stand beside him.

"No, what?" He shook his foot ever so slightly.

"Were you able to get the toxicology reports you told me about?" she asked.

Sure his body was not going to give his thoughts away, he turned back to her. "I haven't gotten a chance to look yet. We just got done with our report." He motioned down the hall. "My office is this way. If you're going to ride with me today, I need you to fill out some forms.

And to be honest, it's been so long since I've had a rider with me—I assume you'd want to tag along on the case—that I don't even know where the forms are. It may take me a minute to get everything together for you."

He actually couldn't remember the last time he'd had someone outside law enforcement ride with him. It had to have been when he was working patrol, but that had been almost three years ago.

She blushed. "I'm glad you thought enough of me to want to let me join you, then. I thought that what we were doing…it was something you did. You know, joint task force–style."

He gave her a half grin. She wasn't wrong— he did work with a variety of people, but normally they didn't hang out while doing their jobs. "I do work with others, but working with private contracting groups is a new one for me. Trained with you guys before at the Special Operations Association for the state, but that's about it. We don't often cross paths." He walked into his office and she followed behind. "Feel free to take a seat."

She cleared her throat, like she was trying to dispel some of her nervous energy, or that could have just been his wishful thinking.

Landing on his email, he found the latest from the medical examiner. Clicking on the file, he opened up the complete autopsy reports. "Yep. Looks like we got everything back on Catherine," he said, looking over at Elle. "And, by the way, just to cover our bases…whatever I tell you, it needs to stay between us."

She frowned. "That shouldn't be a problem, just so long as I can let my team in as well—at least, if need requires. Will that be okay?"

"As this is an open investigation, I'm afraid there may be things that I can't tell you. But what I do tell you, you can give to your team… if need requires."

She nodded, but from the tight expression on her face, he could tell that she was slightly annoyed that he couldn't just give her all the answers. He wished he could, if it would make things easier on her. Yet, in his world, there were too many prying eyes and ears and few people he could trust. If something got leaked about this case, something that he had told her, and the kidnapper got off on a murder charge because of Grant's misstep, he wouldn't be able to forgive himself.

Though he was certain that Elle wouldn't do anything or say anything to intentionally cause problems, it was the littlest cracks in a case that could cause them to crumble or implode. And there were few things worse than watching a person he knew was guilty walk for a crime they had committed.

And that was *if* they got their hands on the person or people responsible for Catherine's death and Lily's disappearance. Right now, it was one hell of an *if*, and it just kept getting more precariously unattainable with every passing hour.

He clicked open the file and stared at the pictures the ME had sent over. Catherine's body was exposed. In the woods, he could tell she had been stabbed repeatedly. Yet, seeing her cleaned up and naked, the savagery took on a whole new level. There wasn't any part of her that hadn't been touched by a blade. Whoever had come after her had even sliced at the back of her ankle.

Had they been trying to cut her so she couldn't run away? Had she been trying to run?

From the multitude of wounds, the killer had to have been full of rage—as he had first assumed. Yet who could have been this angry with the woman?

He looked at the picture of Catherine on her side, her back exposed. She had at least fifteen stab wounds to her torso, one just where her kidney was located and another over her heart. Either of them would have been enough to end her life.

One thing most people didn't realize was how slowly a person died. There were only four things that could instantly end a person—a stabbing wasn't one of them. Which meant that, for at least a few moments, Catherine had to have known what was happening to her and that she was likely experiencing her last moments.

The thought made a chill run over his skin.

Maybe she had been fighting, and that was what had caused the rage. It made sense. She had been off the trail when they found her. Maybe she had broken free and the attacker had tried to catch her, cut her Achilles tendon to slow her down. Maybe she had run and hidden under the tree, but the killer knew she wasn't long for the world. That order of events, that made sense...finally. He had an answer as to how she had ended up where they had found her.

He clicked on the picture of Catherine's arms. On the back of the forearms were the bruises and slashes consistent with defensive wounds. She had been fighting.

Good for her.

It was a strange relief to know that this woman hadn't gone down easily. She hadn't won, but she hadn't just given up, either. There was an incredible amount of bravery in her end, one that he appreciated. If only her fight could have been enough, at least enough for them to have found her before she passed.

Unfortunately, he hadn't made it to her in time.

And that, that inability to save everyone who needed his help, was one of the hardest parts of his job.

"Are you okay?" Elle asked, and he realized she was staring at him. He had no idea how long she had been watching.

He pinched his lips. "Yeah. I'm fine. From the looks of things, Catherine fought hard."

Elle sent him a tired smile. "That doesn't surprise me. I just hope that we can work fast enough that her daughter doesn't have to."

He nodded, unable to look her in the eyes. Scanning the document, he paused as he spotted something in the section about Catherine's clothing. There, it read:

Blood located on upper arm of gray coat. Two-square-inch sample removed and analyzed. Using a precipitin test, it was found blood was human. Blood was type O pos. Deceased was found to be AB positive. As such, blood was not that of the deceased. Further DNA testing is required. Sample sent to state crime lab in Billings.

He wasn't sure whether or not he could give the information to Elle. On one hand, it was intriguing; clearly there were multiple people injured. But what if the injured party wasn't the attacker, but was Lily?

Such information could set Elle over the edge.

"Do you happen to know Lily's blood type?" he asked.

Elle frowned. "No, why?"

"Just curious." He could probably get his hands on that information by the end of the day. At the very least, perhaps he could find out if the other blood was the same type. If it wasn't, they could still hang on to the hopes that the little girl was still alive.

Chapter Nine

She couldn't handle sitting there in his office and doing nothing. Elle had never been one for inaction, and ever since she had gotten off the mountain, she had been working on finding Lily. Her boss at STEALTH, Zoey Martin, had put all their tech gurus on task, running drones, LIDAR and every other thing they could to scour the mountain. Then she had them go over every flight record in hopes that they could track down the child.

Unfortunately, even with all of the professionals on their team and their abundant resources, they had come up empty-handed and Elle had ended up sitting here, as hobbled by the sheriff's department and the crime lab's response time as she was by her team's lack of information.

Grant's face was stoic, but she noticed him read something and then move in closer to the screen, making her wonder if he was having a hard time seeing something and needed readers or if he was just focusing hard on something she couldn't see. He was too young for readers, so he had to be focusing. Was it to do with Lily's blood type?

After he had asked her about it, everything in him had seemed to shift. It was like watching Daisy. When she was looking for a scent, she would weave right and left, working the area. Yet when she picked it up, her whole body shifted; she went rigid and the weaving stopped.

Just by watching him read, she could see his weaving had stopped. Grant had picked up a scent.

Unfortunately, he had made it clear that he was only going to give her information on a need-to-know basis. She wished he would trust her and open up, but at the same time she could completely understand the nature of his job. His inability to give her information wasn't really about her, or any of her failings. There were parts of her job that she wouldn't have shared with him, either. Yet it didn't change the fact that it sucked. Lily's life was on the line, and here they were having to play the game of politics and secrets.

She sent a text to Zoey. If anyone could get their hands on Lily's blood type, it was Zoey. She could probably either personally hack a hospital's records system or have one of her team members do it before they even left the office. What that woman could do with a computer was impressive.

In fact, she could probably get into Grant's computer right now. Sure, law enforcement and the courthouse likely had several layers of cybersecurity, but that didn't make them impenetrable. As quickly as the option came to mind, she brushed it away. Whatever was in that report, she would come to learn it on her own. Zoey didn't need to get into more trouble than absolutely necessary.

In fact, she had an idea, and better, she wouldn't have to call in the big guns.

"How do you feel about HIPAA guidelines?" she asked, giving Grant a mischievous grin.

He scowled, but the action was sexy and only partially judgmental. "Why?"

"How badly do we need to know Lily's blood type? Is it critical or just a curiosity?" She silently begged for it to be the latter, just some potentially inconsequential detail that had only a minor bearing on their case.

A pain filled his eyes and moved straight into her core. "It could be pretty important."

She nodded, looking away from him out of fear that if she continued to meet his gaze, what little control she had over her fluxing emotions would collapse. "Then I'm on it."

She picked up her phone and pulled up the email Catherine had first sent her when she had agreed to take on Lily's security detail. There, she found the numbers and information she was looking for. She dialed the pediatrician's office, and a secretary answered. The woman sounded cloying and chipper, at odds with every part of Elle's current existence.

"Hi, Mary," she said, regurgitating the woman's name in the same chipper tone in hopes it would soften the woman up to the ask she was about to make. "My name is Catherine Clark, and I'm calling about my daughter, Lily Clark."

"Hello, Mrs. Clark, so great to hear from you. How can I help? Is Lily doing okay?"

Grant's eyes were wide with surprise, and her mischievous grin widened into a dark smile. Sometimes the best part of living in small communities was the inherent trust that came with it; fortunately for them today it could be used to their benefit—hopefully.

"Lily is just fine," she lied. "I was just filling out some paperwork for an upcoming summer camp, and I was wondering if you could provide me with some information I have missing from my records. Would you be able to do that?"

"Hmm." The secretary paused, as if she was considering what information she was willing to give. "What kind of info do you need?"

"First, we would need her vaccination records," she lied, trying to think of what reasonable things a camp would need in order to sell her real ask. "Also, it looks like they have a question about blood type, as well. Would that be on record?"

The woman tapped away on a keyboard in the background. "Can you give me her date of birth?"

Elle rattled it off, thanking the real Mrs. Clark for being the ever-so-uptight mother—at least when it came to hiring the help—and also thanking law enforcement for not yet releasing the information about the murder and kidnapping to the media. Otherwise, Mary wouldn't be dealing with her.

"If you like I'd be more than happy to email this information over to you," the secretary said.

"That would be great," she said, giving the woman her encrypted email address that she used for STEALTH. "By chance, did we have her typed and crossed?"

"Yep," the woman said, "looks like she is O positive. Don't worry, I will go ahead and attach those results to the email, as well."

Elle smiled as she thanked the woman and hung up the phone. She looked over at Grant, her smile so wide that it was actually starting to pinch at her cheeks. "It is amazing what a mom can accomplish in five minutes. I don't know if you are aware, but being a mom may actually be kind of magic."

He nodded, but there was something wrong about him. Her smile disappeared.

"What's wrong, Grant?" She slipped her phone back into her purse.

"She's O positive?" he asked, a strange pleading tone to his voice almost as if he was hoping that he had heard the secretary wrong.

"Yeah, why?" There was a long pause, and with each passing second, her body clenched harder and harder, threatening to collapse in upon itself. What wasn't he telling her? What did he know? "You have to tell me what is going on here, Grant. You can't leave me in the dark."

He looked up at her, and she could have sworn there were tears in the corners of his eyes, but as quickly as she noticed them, he blinked them back. "The examiner found some blood on Catherine's sleeve. Blood that didn't match. It came back as O positive." His voice thinned as he spoke, becoming almost unintelligible.

She swallowed, hard. Lily had been injured…

Elle slumped back into the chair as the news flooded through her senses. She brought her hands to her mouth, chewing on the edge of her fingernail.

Lily was out there, hurt somewhere. She was

sitting here and doing nothing. Yet, what could they do? Who could they talk to that would know anything, that could lead them to her?

Futility. This was pure hell.

Grant moved to come closer to her, like he wanted to somehow take back the words he had said to her, but the findings weren't something he could control. This wasn't his fault. None of this was his fault—it was all hers. She put her hand up to stop him from moving closer, and he sat back down in his chair across the desk from her.

He looked dejected. Had he needed to be consoled just as she did? Or was his need to comfort her for her alone?

Right now, it didn't matter. Nothing mattered but getting Lily back.

"Grant," she said, her voice hoarse from the silence and stress.

"Hmm?" he asked, watching her.

"I can't just sit here and hope to find answers."

He nodded, sadness marking his features. "I know. But there are only so many doors we can knock on to get answers. This case, it's proving to be far more complex than what we had initially assumed it would be, especially with federal law enforcement involved. It's been hard getting anyone to answer our calls in DC, let alone share much beyond what we already know. According to the feds, the senator has had the usual string of death threats, and he'll share those with us when we see him. I hope you know I have been stopping at nothing to get Lily home."

He grabbed some papers as they spit out of the printer and handed them over to her, waivers for her to ride along. She signed them and slid them across his desk. "Can you print out the autopsy findings, too?"

His eyes darkened, and he shook his head. "I can answer questions and give you information, but that could get me into some hot water."

She sighed, but she couldn't pretend that she didn't understand the whys and hows of his thinking. "Fair. But what else did they find? Is there anything? Did they ever manage to get into her phone?"

"iPhones are known for being ridiculously hard to get into without a password. I was hoping that when we meet up with Senator Clark he would give us that." As he spoke, he glanced down at his watch. He picked up her signed forms and stuffed them into the basket on his desk. "In fact, we need to head his way."

She didn't want to stay here and be helpless, but she didn't really want to go and question the senator, either. The good news was that he probably wouldn't even know who she was, as they'd never met each other in person, but that wouldn't stop the growing dislike she held for the man.

How could it have taken him so long to get back to the state when his *daughter* was missing? She would have taken advantage of every possible resource—hell, she *had been already*, to help Lily.

Grant stood up and pulled on his jacket. "His plane, if it's on time, should be arriving in fifteen minutes."

"Do you really think he is going to freely give us information? And you know whatever he has to say, it will be nothing but lies." She felt the fire on her tongue as she spoke.

Grant glanced over at her, his eyes widening. "I take it you don't like Dean Clark?"

She shrugged. "I don't like him or his political ads, but in reality, I don't even know him. He is never with his daughter. In the months I have been working there, I have not once actually seen him in person, let alone heard Lily talk about him. I honestly couldn't tell you one time that she said the word *Daddy*."

He checked his utility belt and then stepped toward the door, motioning for her to walk ahead of him. "That's interesting. You ever have any idea why he is so distant?"

"From the family or from Lily?" she asked, walking into the hall as he closed up and locked the office behind them.

"Both, either… I'm curious. I don't have any kids, but if they didn't talk about me, I would take it pretty hard. I would like to think most men want their children to love them." They made their way out as they spoke.

"Not all men want to be fathers, and I think it's fair to assume he is one only because then he can pull constituents from the suburbs. If he is anything like Catherine, you know what he is focused on—and it most certainly isn't actually being the person he pretends to be." As she spoke, all of her secret and pent-up feelings about the family came boiling to the surface.

In fact, she hadn't even realized she had been thinking such things, and yet there they all were coming out of her mouth like she had opened up some kind of fire hose full of unspoken opinions.

Grant was silent as they made their way outside and to his truck. He opened up the door for her, and as she climbed in, she couldn't help feeling as though she had perhaps said too much and had come off as something and someone she wasn't. She didn't hate Dean or even wish him ill; she just couldn't understand him.

As Grant closed the door and walked around

the other side, she watched him move. His coat was stretched tight over his shoulders, and for the first time she noticed how wide they were and how his body was the perfect V-shape of a man who worked out. He stopped and picked something up, and as he moved, she couldn't help but stare at his round ass. That ass. Damn. He must have been the master of squats.

The animalistic part of her brain, the part she wished she could control, made her wonder how it would feel to have him in between her legs. She could almost feel his ass in her hands as he made a few of her wilder fantasies come true.

Maybe it was the tension of the case that turned her thoughts to carnal pleasures and away from the grimness of reality.

What would it be like to feel his breath mix with hers? To have him whispering all the things he wanted to do to her in her ear?

She shifted in the seat, trying not to let her thoughts reach her body but already knowing that there were some things—just like her thoughts about Grant—that she could not control.

It had been incredible just to kiss that man. Yet things had gone all kinds of wrong when they had. It was up in the air as to what would happen if they were ever to try again, but damn if she didn't want to.

She licked her lips as he got in, and she sucked at her bottom lip before letting it pop out of her mouth as she gave him one more sidelong glance. He started to look over at her, and she quickly glanced away. He didn't need to know the thoughts she was experiencing about him right at this moment. If he did…well, she didn't want to know where it would lead. At least not yet, not right now.

Maybe if they finally found Lily and put Catherine's killer behind bars, then she could focus on getting back into the dating world. Her loneliness could have been the driving force behind everything she was feeling when it came to Grant.

There were a million reasons they couldn't be together. First and foremost, that they worked together—but that wouldn't be a permanent thing. And well, for all intents and purposes, she didn't really *know* him. She wasn't the kind of woman, or at least she didn't think she was the kind, who fell head over heels for a man after having just met him. She was far too methodical for that kind of nonsense. Then again, Daisy had approved, and that spoke volumes about what kind of man he was.

"Lily is going to be okay. It's all going to be okay," he said, looking as though he wanted to reach over and touch her once again.

He kept doing that. "Why don't you want to touch me?" she asked, looking down at his hand.

He balled his fingers into a fist and then extended them toward her. "I want to. Believe me, I *really* want to touch you, but I have to be careful. In my job, if we lay hands on someone, those folks are going to jail."

She tilted her head back as she laughed. "Well, then don't touch me. I have shit to do."

Now he was the one laughing, and she ate up the rich, baritone sound of him cutting up. That would be an amazing way to spend a day, in his arms and listening to that sound.

She reached over and extended her hand to him, palm up. "If you promise not to arrest me, I think we can try this thing."

He slipped his hand into hers, pulling their palms tight. It felt secure there in his grasp, and the image of him bending over and all the things she wanted him to do to her body flashed through her mind.

"I'm glad you wanted to touch me again. I was afraid that I had scared you away." He smiled at her.

That smile…she wasn't sure which part of him she liked best. His eyes pulled her into their medley of colors and lines, but then he spoke. Even his voice…oh, his voice.

"You are something special, Ms. Spade." He

lifted her hands and gave her a soft kiss to the back of her knuckles.

Her legs tightened together, giving away all the places her body was responding to his lips on her skin. She didn't know what to say to him. Did she compliment him back, or would it be too forced and inauthentic? But she couldn't just say nothing—maybe she should say thank you, but if she did that, would she seem like a narcissist?

"Thank you," she said, smiling at him. Self-love and knowing her self-worth wasn't narcissism, it was power. And damn it, she wasn't a doormat.

It felt strange and wonderful to claim her power and go against so many of the life lessons that had been thrust down her throat as she had grown up. Her mother had been a powerhouse and her father had been supportive of having a wild child as a daughter, but it was ridiculous how the world worked to stuff a woman in the submissive patriarchal box. If a woman didn't cook for her man, she was lazy. If she liked sex, she was a whore who must have been with hundreds of men. And if she could see the power in herself, the fire within her, she was a stuck-up brat.

His smile widened. "It's nice to hear a woman accept a compliment for once."

She forced herself to look over at him instead of coyly looking down at her hands. "Well, I appreciate you telling me what you are thinking and feeling. Seriously, it is amazing what two people can accomplish if they actually just say what they are thinking and feeling to one another—at least in the way they can."

His grip loosened. "I'm sorry about that. That I can't give you everything you want in the investigation."

Crap.

"That's not what I meant, not at all. I just meant in life." She squeezed his hands in hopes it would reassure him. She wanted to explain it more, to tell him all the things she was thinking and how she wasn't the kind to be intentionally rude or cruel, but they were pulling up to the terminals.

"It's fine," he said, letting go of her and putting the truck into Park. "I'm just glad I get to touch you, at least once in a while."

She felt the heat rising into her cheeks, but she wasn't sure what had caused it, his sweetness or the thought of his skin pressed against her again.

How could this hard-edged, stoic man who had intimidated her when they first met be such a soft-hearted guy when they were alone? He was full of contradictions, but damned if she didn't have a growing need for what he was offering.

Like a true gentleman, he came around and helped her out of his truck. She cleared her throat as she tried her damnedest to stay cool. It was possible that his being a gentleman was a result of his job, and likely a habit of cuffing and stuffing. The thought made her giggle lightly.

"What are you laughing about?" he asked, closing the door behind her.

"Nothing." *And everything.* How had she found herself holding hands with a man she could have sworn was hotter than the surface of the sun?

If he knew all the things she had done and seen, she had a feeling he would accept her for them. And yet, the thought of being with someone in their field—door kicking, so to speak— made her somewhat uncomfortable. Could two people in their world really work? She could be a bit manic about her job, and she had a feeling he could, too.

He hadn't even called her for two days after their night in the woods. That had to mean something, didn't it?

The doors at the front of the terminal opened, and a good-looking man with graying hair at his temples came sauntering out in a barely mussed Armani suit.

Though she had never met the man, she would have known Dean Clark anywhere. She had seen his picture over the fireplace every morning since she had started this job, and his photo ran in campaign ads. And damned if he didn't look exactly like the oil painting of him and his family.

As though he could feel her staring at him, he glanced over at her and their eyes met. In the cold steel blue of his, she could see she may have finally found answers.

Chapter Ten

Senator Clark was exactly the man Grant would have expected him to be after having watched him on the news over the years. He'd once heard gossip that the senator had opposed a Veterans Affairs funding bill for a new hospital, but then when the bill passed and funding was granted, he made sure to show up on the day they broke ground—nothing like a photo op at the expense of truth.

The senator swept back his pomaded hair as he spoke to a woman who was beaming up at him when they walked out of the terminal together. He smiled, and Grant wasn't sure he had ever seen a more lustful, flirtatious gaze on any woman. If only the woman knew the truth—that the man she was talking to had come back to Montana because his wife had been murdered.

If anything, at least the senator had just moved himself firmly into the number one position on Grant's list of suspects.

Grant gritted his teeth but smiled as he made his way over to the man. "Senator Clark, I'm Sergeant Anders. We spoke on the phone." He normally would have extended his hand in a show of respect to those he was working with, but he had a hard time acting congenial when the senator had been so damned hard to get in touch with.

The senator kissed the woman on the cheek and slipped something into her purse as he bade her farewell, then he finally turned to Grant. "Hello, Anders. I thought we were going to meet at my hotel?"

His hackles rose and he started to say something, but the man cut him off.

"Regardless, I do appreciate just getting this all taken care of as quickly and as efficiently as we can. I need to get Lily back and find justice for my wife," the man said, a look of concern finally flickering over his features.

Grant wondered if his reaction was nothing more than a staged response and a canned script. He hated to have hope this man was genuinely concerned for his wife and child.

"I'm glad you feel that way, sir," he said. "If you wouldn't mind, perhaps we can find a quiet corner in the airport and we can chat." He motioned back inside.

The man was wheeling a small carry-on bag,

and as Grant spoke, he looked down at it as if he was put out that he would have to be seen dragging around a suitcase for any amount of extra time. "Do you mind if I put this in my vehicle?"

He wasn't sure that he could trust the senator to come back, so instead of merely letting him go, he motioned toward Elle. "Sure thing. I could certainly stretch my legs, as well. Nothing quite like sitting in a truck or behind a desk and making phone calls all day." He tried to sound jovial, nonescalatory in any way.

Dean looked over at him and smiled, but it was just as fake as the man it belonged to.

Insincere people, especially those like politicians who used phony concern as a campaign tactic, were hard to read. It made getting information incredibly challenging—and this case would be no exception. The honey and the wax would be inseparable.

Elle walked closer and looked to him. As she did, he realized the senator and Elle didn't actually know one another. How could the man not even know whom he had hired to take care of his child?

"Senator, this is Elle Spade. She is the woman who was hired to help protect your family." As he spoke, Grant nearly bit off his tongue as he realized what he had said and the unintentional burn his words may have left. "She works for STEALTH."

The senator stopped and looked her up and down, like he was taking her all in before choosing his words. If only Grant had taken the same time. He mouthed "I'm sorry" to Elle, but she just shrugged. Her simple action only made him feel that much worse. Of course she was probably beating herself up for what had happened, and then he had gone ahead and made it all that much worse.

"I'm sorry about what has happened, Senator Clark. Please know that I offer my most sincere condolences. Your wife was a remarkable woman," Elle said, bowing her head in sympathy. "I would have never left your home that day if I had known what was going to take place after I had gone."

The senator put his hand on Elle's shoulder, and she tensed under the man's grip. Though the action looked as if it was meant to ease her guilt, there was something insincere about the gesture. Or perhaps Grant was just picking up on what he wanted to see. He didn't like the senator, but that didn't necessarily mean that at his core the man was a monster—or at least more of a monster than any other human being.

Grant's mind wandered to all the things he had seen on the job and the saintlike people who turned out to be the greatest monsters of all and the dangerous-looking biker types who went out of their way to work with law enforcement to stop crimes from happening. Assumptions could be obstacles when it came to finding the truth.

"Thank you, Ms. Spade." The senator squeezed her shoulder. "Know that I don't hold you or your team responsible for what has happened. This was my own mistake. I wish I had told Catherine she required twenty-four-hour protection."

Elle looked even more surprised than Grant felt. The man couldn't have been this kind or understanding. Yet, there he was. Was Grant wrong about him?

Grant watched the senator's features, hoping to read any kind of details the man might give away in his body language. "Why *did* you hire protection?"

"I had been receiving threats. The Secret Service was aware and offered to protect my wife as well as myself, but she refused. She found my job and all these things, safety hazards included, to be invasive." The senator started walking again.

Elle nodded as she walked beside the senator. "She had mentioned that to me on occasion."

The senator gave a thin smile, but it quickly disappeared. "Catherine has always been a stubborn woman. No amount of my talking could convince her to take these threats seriously. She wasn't naive, but she really felt that by living in Montana we would be kept away from the big-city dangers."

Grant nodded. "Do you have a record of any of these threats? Any you think are more credible than others?"

Senator Clark took out his phone as they walked. "What's your email address? I can send you exactly what I sent the Secret Service. I'm surprised they haven't shared it with your team."

Grant wasn't surprised. Federal agencies often had communications and turf issues. It would have been nice if the senator had greased the skids on that.

He handed the man his card. "You can send the information here."

"Great. Just give me a moment." The senator didn't even slow down as he typed away on his phone. "There you go, will be to you in a moment."

They came to the long-term parking, and Grant stopped walking. "I'll wait here for you while you put your bag away." He lifted his phone slightly.

"I'll be right back. I'm happy to give you as much time as you need to go over all the details. However, I do have some other meetings this evening." He glanced down at his watch. "Actually, I have one with the local media outlets starting in just an hour, and I was hoping to clean up before I met them."

"Sir, I mean this in the most professional way, but I would like to think that should I need you to answer questions about your wife's murder and your daughter's disappearance, I will take priority."

The senator smirked. "Oh, they are my number one priority. They always have been and Lily always will be. However…my job doesn't stop because of events in my personal life. This state and the people within it depend on me and my delegation. I must be able to perform to my greatest abilities. I may only be in this job a few more months before the election is over, and I have people breathing down my neck to make certain things happen."

"People who would use your wife and your family's safety as a card to get you to do what they wanted?"

"Perhaps this is me being as naive as my wife, but when it comes to my world, there are certain things that good, moral people won't do. As you will see in that email, the people who have threatened me are not the kind of people you would call *upstanding*. These are folks who have issues." The senator twisted his bag, clearly annoyed at being held back from being able to do exactly as he wanted.

"Hmm," Grant said, but Elle was giving him the side-eye and he didn't have a clue what it meant. "Let me look things over."

The senator dipped his head in acknowledgment. "I'm parked not far from here."

As he walked away, the only sounds were of the fellow travelers who were chatting away in the parking lots mixed with the scraping sound of plastic suitcase wheels as they ground against the pavement. Oh, he knew that sound entirely too well.

Elle stood beside him as he pulled up the senator's email. "You watch him, make sure he doesn't get lost."

She nodded.

"Did you know about the death threats?" he asked.

"Catherine didn't mention them, but I assumed there had to be something going on—why else would they have called STEALTH? We aren't cheap, and we don't take contracts for people who don't have legitimate safety concerns." Her head was on a swivel, as she must have been monitoring the senator.

He scrolled through the email, which read as though it had been drafted by a lawyer even though it had been sent from the senator's personal account. In the email, he mentioned three possible threats, and with each person of interest he had provided a picture and evidence of the direct threats. One was an audio recording of a voice mail left on the senator's personal phone by a man who called himself Jazz Garner.

He wished he was in his truck so he could listen to the audio and run the names through the database, but it would have to wait.

The next was an email sent by one Philip Crenshaw. He was wearing desert tac gear and a shemagh wrapped around his neck. There was a gun in his hands, but he wasn't displaying a flag or patches on his gear. He was standing next to a mud house, similar to those Grant had seen in pictures of the Middle East. If he had to guess, the guy looked like a contractor. But what contractor would send a senator a death threat? They weren't the kind to threaten, they were the kinds to kill—with no one being the wiser.

Strange.

He pulled up the email. The spelling was poor and the grammar was worse, but the message was clear—if Senator Clark didn't vote for the bill SB 102, there would be hell to pay. Grant had heard of the bill, but he couldn't recall what it was about.

Regardless, he wasn't sure why this had been

deemed a credible threat. Yeah, the guy looked intimidating, but without seeing the man's picture it wasn't an email that would have made the hair rise on his arms.

The last threat was from one Steve Rubbick. Another email. In this one, the man had cited neo-Nazi propaganda before writing, "...you and your wife will feel my wrath. I will cut you down like the sheep you are and mutilate your corpse while I make her watch..."

The man went into details, listing things he planned to do to Catherine that made Grant's skin crawl. This man had put time, thought and rage into his threat. Grant could understand why the senator would have taken note. The only thing that wasn't listed was where the man intended to kill them or the senator's home address. Either the man hadn't known it or perhaps his letter was nothing more than a rant by a madman.

More than the details or even the diatribe of whys, it was the rage that drew Grant's ire the most. Catherine had been stabbed more than seventy-three times in total. That kind of overkill was something that was only done in a heightened stage of emotional turmoil.

With murderers he had interviewed in the past, when they committed homicides like this, they talked about going into an almost trance-like state. They found pleasure in the method, pulling the trigger and focusing on the muscles in their fingers and the smell of the spent gunpowder, or when stabbing, they found a rhythm in their motion and lusted after the sensation of the point piercing the skin, slicing through muscle and glancing off bone.

"Anything?" Elle asked.

"Definitely some things to go off." He pulled the picture of the contractor on his phone. "How long have you been active in the contracting world?"

She shrugged as she stared out into the parking lot. "I dunno, more than five years now, why?"

"One of our possible suspects is a contractor, or was one." Asking her if she knew this guy was like asking someone from New York if they knew another New Yorker; the chances were almost nil. Yet, he had to check. He lifted his phone for her to see. "Do you recognize this guy?"

Elle reached over for his phone, not letting her watch on the senator down. She glanced at the photograph on his phone. Her gaze flicked over the image and she looked up, but a second later she looked back at it and stared.

"So, you do know him?" he asked, surprised.

"I didn't know he was a contractor." She

frowned. "But he is one of the guys who was with Catherine the day she was killed."

Holy shit.

It couldn't have been that easy. No way. Yet, these stars aligned. Finally, they had gotten their break. They would have gotten it earlier if the senator had bothered to work with the locals.

SHE FLIPPED TO the next photo on Grant's phone. Elle's breath caught in her throat. This man in the photo collage from the senator had also been standing in Catherine's living room the day she had disappeared. The photo of the third man, who was identified as Jazz, was the only one of the group she didn't recognize.

The contractor, Philip, was the man she'd seen smoking a cigar. She closed her eyes, trying to recreate the last image she could recall of the living room and where the men had been standing when she'd last seen them. Steve had been across the room with the group of men, but she couldn't recall what he had been wearing or if he had said anything to her.

There was the sound of footsteps approaching in the distance, and she looked up and watched as the senator returned. He had a smile on his face and gave them a small wave. "The email help at all?" he asked.

Grant returned the man's smile and gave him

a stiff nod. "Interesting. We will definitely look into things." He reached into his pocket and withdrew Catherine's cell phone; it was bagged and tagged for evidence. "I was actually hoping you could help me with one more thing before I hit you with too many questions. Do you know the passcode for your wife's mobile device?"

The senator reached up and ran his hand over his neck, unintentionally covering his weak point. He was stressed. Daisy would do the same thing—cower and cover her neck—if she was upset or concerned for her safety. It was an instinctual move, and Elle had even caught herself doing it sometimes. Yet the senator doing it in this moment struck her as odd. Why would opening up his wife's phone make him uncomfortable?

"I don't know if I can get you in, but I guess I could try." He held out his hand. "You think there's anything on there that could help point you in the right direction, as far as possible suspects go?"

"Don't take it out of the bag." Grant handed the phone over. "As you well know, we're just trying to put some pieces together here. We are trying our hardest to get to the bottom of this case and find justice for your wife as well as locate Lily."

Taking the phone, the senator tapped in a series of numbers. He opened it on his third try and, as it opened, he chuckled and handed the phone back to Grant. "The code is 062510. I'm sorry. I thought the feds already gave this to you."

"What is that?"

"Our wedding anniversary." The senator smiled. "Catherine was always a wonderful wife." As he spoke, his voice cracked with emotion.

Grant nodded. "From everything I've heard about your wife from the witnesses we all have interviewed, it sounds as though you were a very lucky man. I am sorry for your loss."

The senator nodded, clearing his throat. "You guys have anything on Lily yet? The last I'd heard your teams hadn't managed to locate anything that could point us in her direction. Is that still true?"

Elle twitched.

Grant put his phone away and rested his hands on his utility belt, masking his badge. "Unfortunately, we are still struggling to find where she could be located. Again, we are looking."

The senator's eyes darkened, and she could tell he was angry. For the first time, she liked the man. But it had taken talking about Lily before she had seen any genuine emotion.

"Would Lily have known any of the men that were referenced in your email?"

The senator balked. "No, what would make you ask that?"

This time, she wasn't sure if the reaction was real. "I was just wondering if you know of anyone who she would have felt comfortable going with. For a while, on the trail, we found her tracks. She had been walking side by side with her kidnapper for almost a mile."

The senator closed his eyes, and his head dropped low. He ran his hands over his face as they stood there in the cold. When he lifted his head, there were tears in his eyes. "You of all people have to know that I've been a shitty father when it came to Lily. I haven't been with her nearly enough. The truth is, I didn't know you—and I should have. If I tell you I know who was coming and going in her life, that would be a lie. And that, that is something I'm not proud of."

She wouldn't have expected those words to come out of the senator's mouth in a thousand years. He was a seasoned politician, and even for a person in that role, the level of candor and humility in his words stunned her.

Grant nodded, and he also seemed to appear to soften to the man. "Senator, we have all made mistakes in our lives. And as much as I wish you could give me the right answers to our questions, I prefer the honest ones."

The senator dabbed at the corner of his eye, collecting himself. "Do you know when they will be releasing my wife's body? I was hoping to take care of her funeral arrangements while I'm in Montana."

"The medical examiner has filed their reports, but there are a few more tests before everything is finalized. However, I think that you can now claim her remains at any time."

"I will let the funeral home know," he said. "In the meantime, if we are done here, I need to see the rest of my family and take care of some business. If you need to ask me more questions, or if things arise that need my attention, please do not hesitate to reach out."

Elle was sure Grant had more questions for the man, and he had to be as put out by his dismissal of them as she was, but Grant didn't say anything.

The senator turned to her and extended his hand. "And I want to say thank you. I appreciate you coming out and working with the local law enforcement in helping to find my daughter. I didn't fail to notice that you are going above and beyond the call of duty."

She appreciated the flattery. "You are welcome, sir. And I promise I won't stop looking for Lily until I have her in my arms."

"I'm sure that is true." The senator gave her a double pat to her shoulder. "Good evening, and again. Thank you both." He turned and walked away, leaving them standing there at the entrance of the lot.

If she had to explain the situation to someone who hadn't been there, she would have had to admit they had just been worked over by the senator. He was definitely a power player in the world of communication. The old adage of "could sell ketchup Popsicles to a woman in a white dress" came to mind.

They watched him pull out of the lot and make his way to the toll booth before Grant finally turned to her. "What do you make of that?"

She shook her head. "I think that if he's who we need to talk to in order to get answers, then this investigation is going to take a while."

Chapter Eleven

Grant tapped away on his computer inside the truck. Elle had gone quiet, but he couldn't tell if it was because she was relieved or upset. She was softhearted, and surely the senator had thrown her for a loop, yet she wasn't giving her thoughts away.

If anything, she looked *okay*. Maybe the senator's words had helped to mollify the guilt she must have been feeling about Lily falling to the family's enemies.

Grant opened the audio file. The sound was poor and the man who was speaking was slurring as he spewed hate for the senator. He didn't mention Catherine.

"Do you want me to look through Catherine's phone?" Elle asked, finally breaking the silence between them. "Maybe I can pull something."

He reached into his pocket and handed it over to her. "Have at it."

They had gotten a warrant after they had sent

a preservation letter to request that the phone company save the data from the phone as well as from the senator's, but so far, he hadn't received the device's text message and call history. With it open, they might not have to wait for the company to get on the ball.

She tapped in the unlock code and flipped through the screens while he turned back to his computer.

He started by running Jazz through the database. The man came up known, but clean. Next, he turned to the contractor, Philip. Nothing came up when he typed the man's name in the database. As a contractor, the man might be using a false name, Grant thought. He ran the name as an alias, but no matter how deeply he searched, he couldn't even pull this guy's driver's license or known address.

His thoughts moved to Elle. Was she the same way? Was her name even Elle? What if she was working under an alias and just couldn't tell him? If she was, so was the rest of her family. The Spades were well-known in the small, local law enforcement community. They and the rest of the STEALTH group were always more than willing to lend a hand or get information when they were in a pinch.

Yet that didn't make what he knew about her any more real or accurate than what he knew about the senator. The realization bothered him, deeply. At the same time, he couldn't condemn her or judge her because of her lifestyle. There were innumerable details that he couldn't give her about himself. Besides, what was really in a name or background information...even in a past? He liked the woman who sat beside him, the woman who wasn't afraid to show her emotions, who worked harder than most people he knew and lived to make the world a better place.

He sat there thinking about everything as he stared at the screen and pretended to read through the list of ongoing and open calls coming from dispatch. "Elle," he said, finally unable to hold back any longer, "do you use an alias?"

She jerked as she looked up from Catherine's phone. "Huh?"

"Is your name really Elle?" He felt sheepish for even asking.

She chuckled. "You finally going to ask? I was wondering if you would."

He shrugged.

"Yes, my name really is Elle. But when I'm not home, I work under any number of names depending on where in the world I will be. Why?"

He was secretly thankful she had trusted him enough to give him her real name.

"The guy you recognized, do you think he's

working an alias right now?" Grant lifted the phone so she could look at the man again.

"If he is on a contract right now, he probably is using a false name." Elle paused for a moment. "And if he was working under an alias, it makes me think he is definitely the man that we should be looking for."

Grant nodded, but he hadn't needed her to point him in the man's direction; he was already there. He typed in the next suspect's name and waited as the computer ground through the data. Several different Steve Rubbicks popped up; they were a variety of ages ranging from eighteen to eighty-four. From the picture, he guessed the guy they were looking for had to be in his late thirties to early forties. Three off the list fit the demographic.

He clicked on the second one, and the man who popped up was a ringer. Same dark eyes and cleft chin. According to arrest records, the man had been locked up for a PFMA, or partner/family member assault, five years ago. Since then, he'd been free of trouble, but in his booking photo there was a swastika tattooed at the base of his throat.

According to his arrest record, his last known address was just outside city limits.

"I have a hit." Grant smiled. "Buckle up. Let's

take a ride out to Steve's place. See if we can find him."

Elle buckled her seat belt, but she barely looked up from the phone. It surprised him that she wasn't more excited, but even he was feeling like this very well could be an ill-fated run. The man had been at the right place at the right time to fall well within their list of suspects, but he seemed like the kind who wasn't about to just roll over and give them the information they wanted. If anything, he looked entirely antigovernment in the way he sneered back from his booking photo.

How had such a man ever even stood in the same room as the senator's wife? STEALTH had been tasked with personal security for Lily, but apparently they didn't have any active roles in monitoring who came and went from the property. And if Catherine wasn't taking the death threats seriously, it definitely made sense that she wouldn't have pushed the security team for that kind of vetting.

It all came back to being from a sparsely populated and isolated state. Around here, there was an inherent trust. And that naive trust had come back to bite the Clarks squarely in the ass. On the heels of his thoughts was his pity for Elle. What a mess she had found herself in—the scandal would undoubtedly mark her career if the public ever caught word of what had led up to Catherine's death and Lily's disappearance.

Even though STEALTH wasn't responsible for the breech, they would be the ones who would find themselves being scrutinized by the court of public opinion. Luckily, the news hadn't really broken too wide. The only thing he'd seen mentioned was that the sheriff's department was investigating a possible homicide. No word of Lily.

But when and if it came out that a senator's wife had been murdered, it was possible that all hell would break loose. He would be getting calls from every Tom, Dick and Harry who would swear they saw something and knew all the answers. And then there would be the mix of people who wanted to both commend or condemn him and his fellow officers for the work they did. It was an understatement to say his hands would be full.

"Do you have any idea what the men were doing with Catherine? Anything at all?" he asked as they drove toward Steve's place.

Elle shook her head. "I have no idea. Besides myself, Catherine was the only woman there and I thought that was strange, but I didn't pay it too much mind given the nature of her husband's job."

"But you didn't hear anything?"

She nibbled at the inside of her cheek. "They were just acting like frat boys, laughing and joking. I don't remember anything that was said, but I would assume that based on how they acted with one another, they likely knew one another fairly well."

"Do you think the men worked together? That they could all be contractors or in the same crew?"

She nodded. "Maybe, but before any are hired, they have to go through a rigorous background check. This Steve guy isn't someone STEALTH would ever consider hiring, not given his radical leanings—that kind of person makes for a hell of a liability."

"I thought you all lived above the law? No offense intended," he added, but she didn't give any indication that she had taken it as anything more than a legitimate question.

"No one is above the law, not even us." She sent him a knowing smile. "Though we do get to run with a looser set of guidelines."

He could imagine, but he'd also seen innumerable headlines about black ops crews that had run afoul of the law—and changed their names and continued on taking care of the business that would always keep them employed. The only people or organizations he had actually heard of being shuttered were the ones who actually did hire people like Steve—the wild cards who got lost in the bloodlust.

If this guy was a contractor by trade and not merely some radical, then they very well could have been walking into a hornet's nest. This guy looked like the kind who would be solidly antigovernment and loaded for bear. He probably was the kind who had a target range in his basement and a bug-out tunnel coming out of a panic room.

Grant had no doubt that if he looked up the man's ATF records, he would find a list of gun serial numbers that would make any revolutionary proud. And that was what the man had bought legally. Who knew how many guns and incendiary devices he had bought from gun shows and out of the back of people's cars? Gun trades were a common thing in all rural communities, but in Montana it was well-known that a person could buy or trade for an unregistered gun within the hour if they felt the need.

In most cases, those kinds of trades and purchases weren't something to be overconcerned about; it was just like any other flea market or garage sale purchase. See a need, fill a need kind of thing. Yet, when it came to radicals, they were the reason that it was frowned upon. In all of his years in law enforcement, there were only a small number of cases in which they had solved a homicide by using a gun's serial number. Most of the time, serial numbers were only used to return stolen guns to their original owners.

As they drove up to the house, there were signs on the trees along Steve's dirt driveway that read Trespassers Will Be Shot in dripping red spray paint on plywood.

"Nothing like feeling welcome," Elle said with a dry laugh.

"It may not be a bad idea for you to stay in the car while I introduce myself to this guy."

Her mouth pinched closed.

"I just want you to be safe. You're only a rider. If you were on duty, I'm sure that you would be more than capable of dealing with this guy," he added, trying to tiptoe around her.

Her scowl disappeared, and he was pretty sure he had even seen her dip her head slightly, as if she was thinking, *damn right*. She was something. He liked that she was soft and hard, lace and leather. He had always wanted a woman like that, one who had the power to take control and face the enemy, and who knew she was a badass who could save herself—but one who still occasionally needed saving.

Right now, she didn't need to be saved, but he could still give her some level of protection against the unknown and potentially dangerous.

The road leading to the house was scattered with potholes and cobbles that made the truck bounce and jump, working his suspension. Why was it that all these societal outliers couldn't take care of their property? Or was it some kind of thing that they wanted to slow any intruder's advance to their front door? In this case, he would have believed the man capable of that kind of thinking. If he was watching them on a closed-circuit camera, then he was probably already grabbing his mags and getting himself ready for a shootout.

Luckily, Grant's pickup wasn't easily identifiable as a police vehicle. It wasn't until a person was up close and personal that they could see the light bar in the windshield that really gave it away. To the layman, it was just another truck, but to this guy... Grant was glad to be locked and loaded.

They came around a bend in the driveway, and the small, boxy house came into view. The place had a corrugated steel roof that was covered in a red patina of rust. The sides of the house were covered with rotting gray wooden siding a few feet up from the ground and then above was torn and faded plastic construction wrap. One of the front windows had been broken, and instead of fixing the glass, the occupants had covered the broken seams with silvery duct tape.

The driveway obviously wasn't some plan to slow; rather, it appeared as though it was neglected out of hardship—just like the rest of the place.

The state of the place was a bit of a shock. Some military contractors made more than $100,000 a year. There were a lot of things a person could do with that kind of money. This man's property didn't give off the scent of prosperity in any way. Maybe he wasn't a contractor after all. Then again, it was also a known thing that when it came to contractors, many had the attitude "earn it to burn it," and that could certainly have been the case here.

It would be smart to look bedraggled from the outside if a person was keeping a gun warehouse behind the walls. Robberies could happen anywhere, but most criminals who were after large hauls weren't going to target a place like this. Then, that could have been thanks to the spray-painted signs, as well.

If he had been on patrol, this would have been one call he would have loved to take. With something like this, at a place that put off the don't-screw-with-me vibe, it was always because there was something interesting and usually dangerous to find.

"I don't feel good about this. Did you let dispatch know that we were heading out here?" Elle asked, running her hands over her hair.

"Don't worry. We will be just fine. Dispatch knows where we are. And you know what to do and how to do it if anything unexpected goes down." He tried to sound unconcerned but wasn't sure he had sold it.

Not to mention the fact that he hadn't actually told dispatch where they would be located. This had been a last-minute, seat-of-the-pants decision to come out here, but dispatch could find him via his phone if they needed to. His phone, just like everyone else's in America, could be tracked with little more than a few clicks of a button.

He pulled the truck to a stop and, with a quick check of his utility belt, stepped out.

"Don't go in the house," she said, still on guard.

The last thing he would do was enter that house, unless things went sideways. "Don't worry, babe, this will be okay."

Though there was no way he could promise anything other than that the future was unknown, she appeared to relax a tiny bit.

He closed his door behind him and looked back at her one more time before he walked up the steps and knocked on the front door. There weren't any visible cameras, but there easily could have been pinhole cameras carefully placed out of sight.

Grant could hear footsteps coming from inside the house. His heart picked up its pace, and he could feel a thin layer of sweat forming on his lower back, but he couldn't allow his central nervous system to kick in right now. He was the one who had to be in control, even in the midst of an adrenaline jolt.

He tensed to listen, hoping that from somewhere inside he would hear the pitter-patter of small footfalls and Lily's little voice calling out to him. Good God, it would feel so good to get this case buttoned up, and then he could think about all the things he wanted to do to Elle.

Beneath the *bomp, bomp* of an adult's footfalls was a strange pattering *click, click, click*.

He had to have been losing his mind or willing things into existence. There was no way in the world that just because he had been hoping to hear Lily's footfalls at that exact moment that he actually was, but then again, fact could be stranger than fiction.

"Hello?" he called, putting his hand on his sidearm.

"I'll be there in a goddamned minute. Hold your goddamned horses. I'm just putting on my pants." A man's voice, raspy and tired, sounded from inside.

The man could take all the time he needed; the last thing that Grant wanted to see was some guy's tally-wacker wiggling about while he asked him some questions. Unless it was like Pinocchio and grew any time he told a lie.

That was terrible.

Yet, he found himself chuckling. At the same time, he couldn't help the little voice in his head that wondered if that man wasn't actually in there putting pants on, but was instead loading a gun and getting ready to shoot him. A push of adrenaline ran through him, making his hands tremble ever so slightly. He squeezed them into tight balls, willing them to come back to fully being under his control.

Control. He breathed out as he knocked on the door again.

This time instead of the man yelling at him, the door flung open. He gripped his pistol, hard. At knee level, a black-and-white goat wearing a hand-knitted purple sweater with a large yellow *A* on it came bounding outside. It bleated at him, and he was sure it was as close to an expletive as a goat could muster.

He had seen some strange shit, but this was a new one. When he looked back, a man was standing in the doorway and smirking out at him. "What in the hell do ya want?" the man asked, spitting on the ground beside Grant's black boot.

Any hopes of getting this on the right foot were now shot.

He paused, taking in the man who was leaning against the door frame and sneering at him. He was balding, with a comb-over, fortysomething, and wore a torn flannel shirt. His hands were beat-up and his knuckles were bruised, but they seemed right at home on the fellow.

"Are you Steve Rubbick?" Grant asked, ever so slightly angling so he was sure that the other man could see the badge attached to his utility belt.

The man's gaze flittered downward to his tin star, and the smirk disappeared. "What the hell do you want?"

"My name is Sergeant Anders from the Missoula County Sheriff's Office, and I was just hoping to ask you a few questions. Nothing too major," he said, trying to put the man a little more at ease.

The man bristled. "We don't need no law out here. You ain't welcome."

He wasn't sure what the man meant by "out here"—they were hardly off the grid, being only a few minutes outside the city, but he didn't dare press that issue. "I can understand you not wanting to talk to me today. I get that you weren't expecting this kind of visit during your day." He spoke unassumingly, trying his best to mirror the man and his speech. "I know when I get a day off from work, the last thing I wanna do is deal with all kinds of nonsense."

The man chuffed. "That ain't no shit." He leaned his body more against the frame, putting his hands over his chest.

At least he wasn't coming at him armed and ready for a showdown. "That's a nice little goat you got there. What's its name?"

The man smiled. He had all his teeth, but as he smiled his neck muscles shifted and exposed the tattoo at the base of his throat. Dollars for doughnuts, the goat's name was Adolf.

"He's Arnie and he's a real dumbass, and yeah, I'm Steve." He didn't extend his hand, but some of the steeliness that he had greeted Grant with had melted off. "That dumbass loves to eat all my goddamned flowers in the spring. Last year, I spent a buncha money on petunias at the store and he ate every damned one of 'em. He's lucky he ain't goat burger."

It was working; the man was letting his guard down and he wasn't even really aware he was doing it. This was one of Grant's favorite aspects of his job—figuring out how to relate to people to get them to open up. People, by and large, were creatures of habit. They ran by a system of social mores and cues that dictated their behaviors until drugs, alcohol or stress affected their judgment.

"I ain't owned a goat. I bet they're a lot of work." He smiled at the man, the action easy and coated with the proverbial butter. "I was always more of a dog person, myself."

The man laughed. "Oh, dogs are good, man. I always had 'em around as a kid, but goats… They the best watchdogs I ever owned. Ain't no one gonna sneak up on me at night with ol' Arnie around."

This just kept getting stranger and stranger, but he wasn't sure he wanted to dig a whole lot more into the man's way of thinking, or else it might dirty his boots. He could empathize all day with odd thinking, but he had to remain objective in order to get this job done.

"I can't imagine who would be sneaking up on you. You got one nice little spread here."

The man puffed up with pride. "I worked real hard getting this place together. I worked for every dime I ever earned, and there ain't no one that is gonna think they're gonna step foot on here and take it away from me."

Though he didn't completely understand the man's ramblings, Grant got the general idea he didn't want to be screwed with. "I bet. What kind of work you do?"

"A little of this and that. I'm telling you, I worked harder than an ugly stripper for each and every dime."

He didn't doubt that for a minute; money was hard to come by for those who weren't born into it in this state. "You look like the security type. You workin' at the mall?" he asked, playing dumb.

The man huffed, clearly a bit put out by his assumption. "Damn, man, what kind of weekend Rambo do you think I am?" He snickered. "I just got back from spending the last six months overseas."

"Overseas, huh? So you've not been around here long? Know anyone named Clark? A girl named Lily?"

The man's eyes narrowed. "Clark's a pretty common name, and like I said, I ain't been back home long. Had a gig in the sandbox."

So, he was likely a contractor. But somehow it just didn't jibe. This man wasn't like any of the other contractors he had ever met. He was more like something out of an FBI video about who not to trust.

"What were you doing over there?" He leaned back a bit, flashing his badge like it had the same effect as truth serum.

The man glanced down, his eyes drawn by his reflexive action. "Well, I ain't supposed to be talkin' about it, but I've been cleaning up a few governmental messes here and there. You know, taking care of business that needs seein' to. That kind of thing."

"You've been contracting for the government, eh?"

The man beamed like he couldn't have been prouder if he had won a gold medal at the dumbass Olympics.

"Which outfit you work for?" Grant asked, giving the man an attaboy bump to the shoulder. "That's some cool shit right there. I got a couple of buddies who have spent some time over there in the sandbox, doing that kind of thing. Good money in it."

The man couldn't have puffed up any bigger or else the buttons on his shirt would have popped open. "Yeah, real good money. But ain't no picnic. You gotta be tough. I seen shit over there…man, there just ain't nothing like it." He stared off into space like he was picking up some memory, likely one that had the power to keep him up at night. That, or he was thinking of a woman. Either way, this man wasn't sleeping anytime soon.

As Rubbick spoke, Grant couldn't help but notice that he had carefully maneuvered around his pressing question. He was probably used to not giving answers, which was something Grant knew a little about himself.

"Who's the woman ya got out there?" the man asked, waving his hand in the general direction of his truck. "She a rider?"

He was a bit surprised Rubbick didn't at least recognize Elle if this was the same person who had been at the Clarks' house. Then, she had said that they had only briefly seen one another, and it was as she had been making her way out of the house. It was more than possible that she had just been a blip on Steve's radar.

"She is a friend of mine," Grant said, trying to sound relaxed and as if her presence was just a normal thing. "I know you can't tell me a whole lot, thanks to the NDAs in your life, but I need to get a few answers to my questions in order to cross you off my list in a murder investigation. You tell me the crew you're working with, and I'd be more than happy to give your boss a call and get you approvals to talk."

The man's eyes narrowed as though he was studying Grant for signs of weakness, but he wasn't about to find any that Steve hadn't already inadvertently pointed out.

"Me and my brother, we're with STEALTH. They are out of Montana here."

The blood drained from his face and Grant

had to put his hand against the house and pretend to lean in order to keep himself from swaying. The man had to be screwing with him. "Excuse me, you and your brother work for STEALTH? What's your brother's name?"

"My brother goes by Ace." The man nodded, sending him a crooked smile. "And yeah, STEALTH's a great crew."

He swallowed back the frog in his throat and tried to keep his gaze from skirting over to Elle. He didn't think the STEALTH crew was large enough to have members, especially in the same town, who didn't know each other. So, one of them had to have been lying to him, but who was it, Elle or this man?

"How long you guys been with that group?"

The man tapped his chin. "I guess it's been about a year now."

"Hmm." He couldn't remember how long Elle had been working with them, but he assumed she had been there for a long time. Maybe he had assumed incorrectly.

Or maybe they were both working for STEALTH but were intentionally kept away from one another and used as a system of checks and balances by their superiors. He'd heard of other organizations, the military usually, that used counterspies as a way to keep their troops accountable and from swaying in the wrong directions.

All the possible explanations he could come up with seemed unlikely, but for the life of him he couldn't wrap his head around everything the man's admission had just done to complicate his case—and Grant and Elle's burgeoning relationship.

Chapter Twelve

When Grant came back to the truck, he was oddly quiet. His eyes were shadowy, and he avoided meeting her gaze as he got in and buckled up. She wanted to ask him what was wrong, but she doubted Grant would tell her.

He slammed the door shut and rolled out of the driveway and onto the main road without a word.

"How did it go?" she asked, already somewhat knowing the answer, but not sure what else to say in order to alleviate the tension which was reverberating around inside the cab of the pickup.

"Fine." He scowled.

Oh shit.

She hated that word. *Fine* could mean a million different things—from calling out a hot woman on Venice Boulevard all the way to being the last word spoken at the end of a relationship.

In this moment, she had a feeling it was the end of something, and she hated the word even more.

"Did he admit to being at the Clarks' place the day Lily disappeared?"

"No." His jaw was set into a hard line.

"Did he know anything about Lily's current whereabouts?" She tried to unlock his jaw with another question.

He shook his head.

She chewed on the inside of her cheek, trying to think of a way to stop whatever it was that was happening between them. What could Steve have said that would have upset Grant like this? Grant hadn't arrested him, so that had to mean that he didn't believe, or at least couldn't prove, the man had anything to do with the crimes.

"Where are we going now?" she asked, hoping what he needed most was just a change of focus and then they could get back to being where they had been with one another before he had gone up to that damned house.

"I'm going to take you to your place. What's your address?" His words were short and hard, and they hit her like stones.

The air in her lungs escaped her as his words struck her. "I… You…" She motioned back toward the man's place. "What in the hell happened back there? We were doing good. We were a team, and now you come in here and act like I'm your enemy."

He let out a long sigh, and it reminded her of Daisy when she was trying to relieve her body of stress. It was funny how people liked to pretend they weren't animals. In all actuality, Daisy was a far better soul than either of them could ever hope to be. All Daisy cared about was loving and pleasing her, through her work and through her play. There were no complications, no games—only love.

"I'm sorry. I didn't mean to be an ass with you. Not my intention. I'm just… I guess I'm trying to sort through some new information. That's all." He put his hand out, palm side up and open and closed his hand like he wanted to hold her hand.

Was that where they were now? Could she hold his hand? Five seconds before he had been furious. Did he think he could just give her his hand and everything between them would go back to being all good?

She couldn't help herself. There were all kinds of pains that could be healed with the complexity that came with a lover's touch. Not that he was her lover—not yet, anyway. And even if his touch didn't fix the weirdness that had come between them, at the very least she wouldn't feel quite as alone. They could navigate this as long as they were in it together, no matter what the world had in store for them.

She slipped her hand into his, and he wrapped his fingers around hers. His hand was so much bigger than hers that he nearly encompassed her completely. She liked that feeling of solidity that came with being touched by a man who was so much bigger than her; he made her feel as if he could protect her from almost anything.

"I know you don't want to tell me what happened, but I hope you know that I'm here if you need anything—even just someone to listen and help you sort through your thoughts."

He twitched as he looked over at her. There was something in the way he stared at her that made her feel as if he was trying to read her for secrets and lies. The warmth and sense of protection in his touch began to dissipate and be replaced with the bitterness of distrust. She tried to swallow back the flavor of it from her mouth, but it lingered on her lips.

He finally looked away. "Where are you staying?"

She tried to pull her hand back, but his grip tightened ever so slightly. "Why do you want to get rid of me?" she asked, trying to say the words lightly when all she really wanted to do was yell at him to just open up and tell her exactly what it was that was bothering him so

much about her. "Why won't you tell me anything about your conversation? Did he tell you
something about Lily? Something bad?" This
wasn't merely new information—this had to be
something to do with them. She could feel it. It
couldn't be about Lily.

He let go of her hand. "Seriously, it's not
about Lily. He…he didn't have anything valu-
able to give us. There hasn't been anything
you've lied to me about, is there?"

"What?" she asked, frowning. "No, why? Did
the guy tell you something, something that is
making you question me?"

He stared out at the road like it was all he
could focus on, but he wasn't blinking. She had
hit on something.

"He did, didn't he?" she continued. "What
did he tell you?"

"I just need to talk to your bosses. That's all."
Finally, he let go of her hand, as though he was
getting as frustrated as she was.

"Why? Please, Grant, talk to me." It felt weak
having to beg him like she was, but she was out
of ideas.

He ran his hand down the back of his neck
and pulled his truck over to the side of the road.

What terrible thing had Steve told him that it
required Grant to pull over in order to talk to her
about it? She had seen cops talk on the phone,

text and work on their computer, all while driving. She couldn't imagine anything that would have made him respond as he was.

"How long have you been working with your team?"

"The Shadow team or STEALTH?"

He shrugged. "Both."

She looked up and to the left as she tried to pull numbers from her memory. "My family and I have been working together, in some facet or another, for the last ten years. We are the only members of the Shadow team right now. As for STEALTH, we've been working for them for a couple of years. Why?"

"Do you know everyone who is employed with them?" he asked, staring over at her as he clenched the steering wheel.

"I know most, but they have contractors that work for them all over the world." She wasn't sure what he was getting after.

"Ah," he said, and his grip loosened on the steering wheel. "So, it's possible that there could be someone working out of here that you didn't know." He huffed. "I gotta say I'm relieved. I thought for sure that you would know everyone working here."

"I do. Or at least I think I do," she said, as what he was implicitly telling her sank in. "Wait, did Steve say he works for STEALTH?"

"Both him and his brother... Ace." He nodded. "I have to wonder if he was trying to screw with me." He chuckled and ran his fingers through his hair. "Not gonna lie, I'm not quite sure what the hell was going on back there. He threw me. I was worried you were hiding something from me. Something that could have screwed this investigation."

A pit formed in her stomach. She wasn't intentionally keeping anything from him, but that didn't mean anything. There could be any number of things he could have needed to know that she had at her fingertips and yet he was just failing to ask.

"I'm not going to hold anything back from you, Grant. I told you, you can trust me."

A smile finally flickered over his features. "You don't know how much that means to me. Seriously. I have to admit, it freaked me out... the thought of you keeping something like that intentionally from me. I guess, without meaning to, I have come to trust you without you ever telling me it was okay. I felt a bit like a fool."

She smiled back. "There are only a few people in this world that I would say I trust with my life, but you are one of them. I feel lucky to have met you." She looked down at her hands, wishing she was still touching him. "But I have to say, you freaked me out, too. I want you to know that whatever you are thinking, just ask. I can't stand the thought of you thinking I'm something I'm not. And sure, I have a lot of secrets and I have made more mistakes and done things others would judge me for, but I don't want to ever have to hide anything from you."

She wanted him to be hers and for her to be his. She didn't know if he wanted the same, but if she didn't put herself out there and take advantage of these quiet and raw moments that seemed so scarce between them, she would regret it later.

"Why didn't you call me after the night in the woods?" he asked, and she couldn't ignore the faint hurt that flecked his voice.

She pressed her palms together as she tried to find the words. "I... I didn't know how to handle that—you. I just was such a mess. And to be completely honest with you, my team and I had been working hard to locate Lily."

"If you had found her, would you have even called me? Or would your team leaders have made the phone call to the department?" There was a note of insecurity in his words, and it made her chest ache.

"I would have called you. I just... I was a mess."

"But you aren't now?" he asked.

Though she was aware he was just trying to

feel her out and measure what she was feeling toward him, she couldn't help but be a little hurt. "I know we've only just started hanging out. But being with you—" she paused, finding her words "—actually, just being *near* you is incredible. You drive me wild. I never, in my wildest dreams, imagined that I would kiss a man in the middle of a job."

He laughed.

"You can laugh all you want," she said, sending him a little smirk, "but I'm serious. I'm normally all business when I'm working. Especially when I have Daisy with me. And with Lily and Catherine, I needed to give them my solid focus, but up there on the mountain, sitting with you... I don't know how to explain it."

"But it felt *right*?" he asked, finishing her thought.

"Yes. *Right*." She smiled as he reached over and took her hand. He drew their entwined hands to his lips and gave her knuckles a kiss. "But it's something more than that. I just can't even—"

"I know exactly what you mean," he said, pulling his truck back on the road.

She wasn't sure that he did, but she was glad they were at least on the same page, a page that could serve as the first of many in building their full story together.

"If you want to talk to Zoey, I'm sure she would be happy to answer any questions you have," Elle said, glad to take some of the pressure off the emotions she and Grant were feeling and trying to navigate together.

She had never completely understood why love had to be so hard. In the history of her relationships, love had never been easy. She had felt love before, but it was something that was so fleeting in her life. If anything, love was a weakness. And maybe that was why she didn't want to talk about it, why they both wanted to push it away and simply focus on the task at hand.

But if they were going to make a go of this thing between them and try and strive for a real relationship, then they needed to talk about the feelings and the weaknesses that came with them. Yet she wasn't sure either of them was ready for that kind of thing. Like they had said, they had only known each other for a short time. In those limited days, love and lust had one hell of a way of looking like each other's identical twins.

After okaying exposing the location of their headquarters to him with Zoey, she pointed Grant in the direction of the Widow Maker Ranch. Sarge, the beloved black gelding who lived at the ranch, was running along the fence line as they made their way to the main house.

Zoey's office was offset from the house in a separate building not far from the stables. In the distance were a series of cabins and row houses. Leading to them was a dirt road, and at the end of it was a flatbed full of trusses, as if they were planning on building yet more cabins or houses.

"I live back there," she said, pointing to the cabin that sat second from the end closest to them. "It's a two-bedroom with one bath, but it fits me perfectly. I was just glad to have my own cabin. A couple of my siblings have chosen to take rooms in the house instead of private cabins." She didn't know why she was telling him all the superfluous details, but she would do anything to make things comfortable between them.

She had no idea why she was feeling so nervous with him—even with their hands intertwined and the acknowledgment that there were mutual feelings between them, she couldn't make her nerves recede. Part of her wondered if it was because of the lingering feeling of his lips on her skin and how badly she wished to feel them again.

"Zoey is probably over there," she said, pointing at the office. "That's our main headquarters. It's where we take reports and have our meetings."

Grant nodded. "But not everyone who works with STEALTH is allowed to be present?"

She shrugged. "No. The main team leaders are normally at most meetings, but folks like me—the grunts—are normally kept out. AJ or Zoey are normally the ones I get my information from."

He nodded and seemed far more at ease.

They parked and made their way over to the ranch's main office. The enormous room was newly constructed and still had the smell of fresh lumber, and it mixed with the ozone smell of the electronics that filled the main area. Zoey was sitting at the far end of the office and swiveled around in her chair as they walked inside. Her hair was purple today, and she had a fresh black tattoo on her neck. "Hey, guys, how's it going?"

Elle smiled. She'd always liked her boss; Zoey was the kind of woman who would not only take no crap from anyone, but she would also make sure that she protected all those around her. If Elle had a choice, she would be just like her when she grew up.

She chuckled at the thought.

"Sorry to bug you," Elle said. "This is Sergeant Grant Anders. He works over at the sheriff's office, and he is helping with the Clark case."

"Ah, I see." The small smile on Zoey's face disappeared, and she searched Elle's face like she was wondering what she had told Grant.

"He has some questions for you."

"Nice to meet you, Mrs.—"

Zoey stood up and stuck out her hand. "Just call me Zoey. I'm not about the patriarchal crap. I may be married and a mom, but no one owns me. My husband and I are partners."

Grant shook her proffered hand. "Nice to meet you. I appreciate you seeing me."

She crossed her arms over her chest, and as she moved, Elle could make out new ink on the top of her breasts, as well. The woman was so cool. Elle had never been one for getting tattoos, but Zoey had her questioning her stalemate on skin art.

"Most of the surveillance team is out for the day, but I should be able to get whatever it is you need," Zoey said, motioning vaguely at the computer screens lining the walls.

"That's great. Right now, though, we were just out talking to one of the men Elle pointed out from the Clarks' place before Catherine disappeared." He glanced over at Elle. "He mentioned that he was working for STEALTH."

Zoey nodded, turning away and making her way back to her workstation at the far end of the windowless room. "What did you say his name was?"

"Steve Rubbick. You heard of him?"

"Hmm. I don't know that name, but you know how it is. These guys could be working under any number of names." Zoey kept her face turned away from them as she tapped away on the computer. "What did he look like?" Finally, she glanced over her shoulder at them.

From the blank expression on Zoey's face, Elle would have said that Zoey was telling the truth about not knowing the man.

"He looks a bit like an extremist. Swastika right here on his neck," Grant said, pointing to the base of his throat.

"Ah," Zoey said. "Well, I don't have to search shit, then. While you can see I'm a fan of ink, I'm not about to hire anyone with gang tats or who are of a questionable moral character." She turned to face them. "I'm proud to say that we only hire contractors who have exceeded our standards and perform at a high ethical level both personally and professionally. We don't want to hire folks we have to monitor."

"Do you know a Philip Crenshaw?" Elle asked, thinking about the frat boy.

"I don't know the name. You have a picture?" Zoey asked.

Grant pulled up a picture of the man from his phone and showed it to Zoey. Zoey choked out a thin laugh. "Yeah, now him…him, I know. He tried to get hired on with us. I handled his interview process. Couldn't have recalled his name, though."

"But he doesn't work for you, I take it?" Grant asked.

Zoey pointed at him. "He had the credentials, but that man was a wild card. He'd had some things in his past that ran a little too far into the legal and ethical gray. I wasn't there and couldn't say if he was right or wrong in making the decisions he did in the heat of the moment, but let's just say I wouldn't have been pleased if he was working for us."

"Do you know where we could locate him?" Grant asked. "I couldn't pull anything up about his last known whereabouts."

"I can see what I can find on him. I will probably have to use the facial recognition software. It may take me a while," Zoey said, pointing at the screens. "You guys have a few hours to burn?"

Elle wasn't sure about what Grant had on his docket, but she hated the thought of not actively searching for Lily. Yet there was little they could physically do without more information—info that was at the mercy of Zoey's tech skills.

"We can hang out for a bit." Grant nodded.

Elle smiled. "I'll just text you their pictures. Maybe you can see if you can pull up anything on Philip."

Grant looked over at Elle. "In the meantime, I'd love to take a look around your place."

That was the last thing she had expected Grant to say, and she could feel her cheeks burning at the thought of being alone with him in her house. At the same time, he hadn't said anything even slightly suggestive.

"Uh, yeah. I'd be happy to show you," Elle said, walking toward the office door with Grant following close behind her.

As they made their way outside, Zoey let out a belly laugh. "You guys have fun. I'll text when I find something. I won't come knocking."

Elle's face burned. Yeah, Zoey definitely worked on a whole different wavelength than she did; she was far bolder.

Their feet crunched on the frozen snow as they made their way across the parking area and toward the row houses. Her arm brushed against her pocket, and she felt the familiar bump of a phone and realized she still had Catherine's cell phone. "Wait." She pulled the phone out of her pocket and showed it to Grant, then held up her finger, motioning for him to wait for her there. "I'll bet she can make something out of this. I'll be right back."

Though she had started to go through the phone, she had found little usable information. The woman had a million contacts and got more texts and phone calls than a retail pharmacy. Elle had gone through what she could in the time she'd had, but given just the volume of information held in the iPhone, it could have taken her days to find anything—let alone anything that would point them toward the killer or Lily.

Zoey was already tapping away when she made her way back into the office. "'Sup? You guys done already? Girl, you work fast." She sent Elle a devious smile.

"We aren't that kind of friends," Elle said, but the burn returned to her cheeks. Just because they weren't those kinds of friends yet didn't mean that she didn't want to see him naked and underneath her.

"Yeah, right." Zoey laughed. "You do know I'm in intelligence, right? Even if I wasn't, I can see the way the two of you look at each other. Remind me not to put you into an undercover role. You can't lie for shit."

"You've put me in all kinds of undercover roles. I did great." She stuck her tongue out at Zoey.

"True as that may be, you can't lie to me about that man," Zoey teased. "Is there something you needed?"

"I forgot," she said with a nod, holding up the bagged phone for Zoey to see. "Here's Catherine's phone. I wrote the unlock code there on the bag." She handed over the phone, pointing at the numbers scrawled in black Sharpie.

"Sweet. I can definitely use this." Zoey gave her a wide smile. "In the meantime, seriously, go and have some fun."

Zoey stood up and shooed her out of the office, but as Elle took one more look back at the computers, she saw Philip's face staring out at her from the screen. His eyes were dark and brooding, far from the jovial man she had last seen smoking a cigar while laughing with Catherine. The man staring out at her looked like a true, cold-blooded killer.

Chapter Thirteen

The little cabin was even smaller on the inside than it appeared on the outside, and Grant could understand why several of Elle's siblings had chosen to take rooms in the main house over these tiny dwellings. It was smart of the STEALTH company to keep their contractors on-site, especially given the nature of their work and the security risks.

Elle's hands were trembling as she pressed the numbers and unlocked the door. He wanted to tell her not to be nervous, that he didn't have anything less than completely honorable intentions on his mind. Yet he was as nervous as she was, and, well, the rest would have been a lie. He had wanted to press her down and make love to her from the moment their hands had touched. But he wouldn't pressure her for anything. If she wanted to be with him, she could lead the show.

Then, she didn't really seem like an aggressive kind of woman. He doubted she would take the lead and make the first moves.

She opened the door and flipped on the lights as Daisy came barreling down the hallway toward them. "Daisy girl!" she said, clearly as happy to see the dog as the dog was to see her.

Daisy dropped down and rolled over in front of them, her tail wagging so hard that her whole entire butt moved right and left on the vinyl flooring. Elle squatted down and loved on the animal as he chuckled. There was nothing sexier than a woman playing with and loving on her dog.

Daisy stood up and finally seemed to notice him; she lunged toward him and rubbed herself around his legs, almost catlike in her excitement. He was slightly taken aback by the dog's warm reaction to his being there, but they had spent a night together taking care of Elle. "Hi, Daisy," he said, squatting down and giving the dog a vigorous scratch behind the ears. "I missed ya, pupper dog."

He caught Elle smiling out of the corner of his eye.

Daisy gave him a big, slobbering kiss to the side of his cheek. Daisy's breath smelled like dog food.

"Oh," Elle said, covering her mouth with her hands. "She's not much of a licker. Sorry about that. If it makes you feel better, she is the ranch dog who is the least addicted to eating horse manure."

"I'm glad." He laughed, but as Elle must have realized what she said, her face turned crimson.

"I, uh…" She ran her hand down the back of her neck and looked toward the main living area. "Obviously, I don't have people out to my place very often. I'm sorry if it's a mess. In fact, I can't say that anyone other than my family has been here." She cringed as she looked at her couch, where a basket full of folded laundry sat ready to be put away.

"Your place is cleaner than mine," he said. "I get two days off a week, and I have to say that I don't really enjoy spending my downtime doing chores. I can't even tell you the last time I mopped a floor. Don't feel bad."

"With Daisy around, if I didn't mop the place, it would be covered in muddy paw prints." She let Daisy outside. The dog bounded away, and Elle looked about, making sure she was safe, then closed the door. "She should be good outside for a little while. She sticks around. Want a drink or something?" She rushed away from him toward the kitchen, as if being close to him was making her even more nervous than she had first seemed when they arrived.

He followed her toward the kitchen. "I'd take

some water, but I can get it." He wasn't sure who was more on edge, her or him. It was as if all the feelings he'd been having for her had culminated into this single moment and he couldn't quite sift through them all.

He walked to the small cabinet by the sink and grabbed a glass out of the cupboard, but before he could fill it with water, he turned around toward her and put the glass down on the counter. "Are you sure you are okay with my being here? We could just go back to my truck or—"

She moved toward him and threw her arms around his neck, and her lips pressed against his. For a second, he couldn't quite make sense of what was happening, but then he wrapped his arms around her and pulled her body against his as he kissed her back. She nibbled at his lower lip, and her tongue flicked against his.

He hadn't pegged her as the dominant type, but he had never been more excited to be wrong. She leaned into him, and though he couldn't tell, it felt like she was even lifting her leg as she tiptoed to kiss him. He slid his hands down from her back and took her ass into his hands. It felt even better in his palms than he thought it would. She had to work out, but not so much that there wasn't the softness that he loved on a woman.

She was the perfect combination of soft and toned, feminine but strong.

He laced his lips down her neck, and her breath caressed his skin in a moan. His body awakened at the sound. He could listen to that sound, the weak moan of a woman in want, forever. His lips found the base of her throat, and he traced his tongue along the hard edges of the little V-shape. She sucked in her breath and held it.

He stopped, taking a moment to look at her. Her eyes were the color of the sky in the middle of a storm, promising a temporary break for the sunshine. "You are so damned beautiful. You know that, don't you?"

She tried to avoid his gaze, but he drew her back with his finger until she was staring at him again. "Don't look away. You don't need to. I want to look at you, all of you." Her gaze drifted to his chest, but he didn't know exactly what she was thinking. "If you're not ready for this, or if you are rethinking things with me, don't worry, you can tell me. We can stop this right here and now. We can just go back to being friends."

Elle reached up and took his hands in hers and finally looked up into his eyes. "No. That's not it. I want you. I want this. I want to do things with you that I've never done with anyone else. I just…"

"You don't feel it?"

She frowned. "What? No."

"Then what is bothering you?" He kissed her hands but kept looking into her eyes.

"I haven't had sex in a long time. I just don't want to be bad." Her hand tensed in his.

He started to laugh but checked himself as she began to pull away. "No, don't go. I didn't mean to laugh. You surprised me, that's all. I thought you didn't want me—I didn't even think you could possibly be feeling insecure about anything. You are the most beautiful woman I've ever known."

"You don't need to lie to me. I know I'm not ugly or anything, but I'm hardly anything special." She looked away again.

He leaned in close and whispered into her ear, "You are something incredibly special to me." He kissed the top of her ear ever so gently. "And I am not concerned about how you are in bed. I think that as long as we are together and we talk, we can be amazing together. You just have to talk to me. Okay?"

She looked up at him and smiled, and there was a new light in her eyes. "It's funny, you telling me that, when that's all I've wanted from you from the very beginning."

"We both have a lot to learn. I will never be perfect—"

"And you know I'm not," she said, giggling.

"You are much closer than I am, but regardless, we can be imperfect together." He kissed her forehead and ran his hands through her hair, pushing it behind her ears and cupping her face. "Well, you can be perfect and I can try to keep up." He kissed her lips gently. "And I promise I will try to talk to you, to tell you what I'm thinking."

She reached up and unbuttoned the top of his shirt. "Right now, all I'm thinking about is how badly I've wanted you."

He smiled wildly. "What do you want me to do to you?"

She looked at him with wide eyes, leaning back in mock surprise. A cute smirk took over her lips. "Take off your shirt." She let go of him and stepped back.

He felt silly, but Elle telling him what to do was so damned sexy, he could have eaten it all up. "As you command," he said, slipping the buttons clear of the holes and leaving his shirt open and loose.

"All the way off," she said.

"Elle." He whispered her name in surprise as he slipped his shirt off his shoulders and let it drop to the floor. He reached for her, but she stepped back playfully.

"What?" she asked, giving him an innocent look. "Vest, too."

He peeled the Velcro straps open and pulled the vest over his head. Then he stripped off the white T-shirt that he always wore underneath.

She sucked in a breath as she watched him, making him smile. That was one hell of a reaction, a reaction he would never get enough of hearing.

"I thought you were feeling out of practice?" he teased.

"That doesn't keep me from knowing exactly what and how I want it. It just means I've had plenty of time to think of all the ways I want to be pleased."

He pressed hard against his zipper. There was just something so sexy about a woman who could talk openly and honestly about sex. If they could say what their hearts desired, then they were probably more than happy to do all the things they wanted to do with their body, as well. And that, that freedom, was something he had always found a great quality in a lover.

She may have been out of practice, but he had no doubts that she was going to be the greatest lover he had ever been with. Then, he had to be grateful for any woman who wanted to give him the gift of allowing him to enter her body.

The thought of slipping inside her, slowly...so

slowly...and watching her face made him feel as if he was going to drip.

"Now what do you want me to do?" he asked, opening his arms and exposing his naked chest to her.

She stepped closer and ran her fingers over the tattoo on his left pec. "What was this for?" she asked, tracing the edges of the black bear paw.

Her fingertips moved slowly along the paw; in their tenderness it reminded him of the pain and reasons he'd chosen to get the tattoo. "One of my best friends was killed in the line of duty. He was shot while performing a routine traffic stop that turned ugly. I got it in his memory, over my heart—I never want to forget that in my world, every day is a gift."

She moved in closer, pressing her body hard against him. "That is beautiful and so true." Her hands slipped down his chest, running over the lines of his stomach and toward his utility belt.

He reached down and unclicked his belt, carefully taking it off so it didn't bump against her. There was nothing worse than dropping that heavy-ass thing on a toe. He threw it on the couch behind them. Before turning back, he glanced at the front windows and made sure the drapes were pulled closed. The last thing they needed was someone walking by and peeking in on what he hoped was about to happen. He needed to protect her privacy as much as he did his own.

"We should take this to the bedroom." He reached for her hand, and she nodded, leading him down the short hallway.

The place was simple, two bedrooms and a bathroom, kitchen and a living area. For his life it would have been perfect. He had to imagine it was for hers, as well.

She slipped the door closed behind them and clicked on a bedside lamp, casting her purple bedroom in a thin light that made everything in the room seem like something out of a burlesque club. He hadn't imagined her bedroom being anything like it was, though he had to admit he had never thought of anything in her bedroom besides her.

There were black satin sheets on her bed, and just like the woman they belonged to, they whispered of fantasies so close to being realized that he was forced to reach down and unzip his pants.

"Take them off," she said, motioning to his pants.

He slid the zipper all the way down and then let them fall to the floor, exposing his gray boxer briefs. She smiled as she glanced at his package, and her expression made his heart leap with joy as he took pride in knowing she liked what he had to offer.

Yet she had no idea. If there was one thing he prided himself on, it was knowing how to please a woman. There was nothing that he would rather do than bring the woman he was with pleasure. He'd heard about men being self-ish lovers, only caring about getting theirs, but what was the point of such behavior? He would get his, that wasn't a question, so why not take joy in the journey of pleasure that two people could experience together?

He'd never understand a woman who stayed with a man who wouldn't try to make sure she enjoyed herself to the fullest. If he wasn't self-less in the bedroom, what made a woman think he would try to make her happy outside the bed-room?

"Where is your mind right now?" she asked, looking up at him with an inquisitive look on her face.

He smiled. "I was thinking about all the ways I want to pleasure you." Reaching over to her, he slipped his hands under the edges of her shirt and slowly pulled it up and over her head, ex-posing her hot-pink lace bra. He felt stupid for thinking she was a blue underwear kind of girl when she stood there wearing this.

If he wasn't already hard enough to cut glass,

the sight of her luscious curves would have done it. If he wasn't careful, he was going to have to apologize for losing control.

"It's your turn." He motioned to her pants.

Instead of listening, she turned to her phone and clicked a few buttons. As impatient as he was for things to continue, he was glad for the reprieve. Chris Stapleton started to play from a Bluetooth speaker she had set up in the corner of the room. This was a girl who knew how to set a mood.

With the beat of the music, she unbuttoned her pants and slipped them down her thighs, pulled them off and threw them on the footboard of her bed. She was wearing hot-pink panties that matched her bra. He'd once heard that if a woman was wearing matching underwear, then they had chosen to have sex when they'd gotten dressed that day. Had she known this was going to happen all along, that they were going to find themselves in a position to share their bodies?

The thought alone turned him on, and in combination with her standing in front of him... *damn.*

A growl rippled from his throat, and he pulled her into his body. He wanted to rip those panties off her with his teeth and then gently kiss every part of her body that the lace had touched.

She gasped as his mouth found her throat, and he cupped her breast in one hand and the small of her back with the other. Every part of her was about to become his.

"Tell me you want me, Elle." He sounded raspy as he spoke her name, and she shivered under his touch.

"Grant, I've wanted you…since the first time we met." She was breathless with want.

"I know that's not true, but I appreciate it anyways," he said with a slight laugh. "I was a dick when we first met, and I'm sorry. But I'm glad you saw past that…that you were patient with me while I found my way to you." He kissed the lace at the top of her bra, taking in the soft scent of flowers on her skin. "To here. To now." He pushed the lace away, exposing her nipple and pulling it into his mouth.

She threw her head back and arched her back as he sucked. He popped it out of his mouth and licked the sensitive nub, then rubbed it gently with his thumb as if thanking it for allowing him the honor of tasting her.

She gasped as he repeated himself on her other side.

He moved his hand between her legs, over her panties, and traced her wet, round mounds until he found what he was looking for. Dropping down to his knees, he pulled off her panties, not wanting to destroy his new favorite article of clothing—one he hoped to see again in the future.

He lifted her leg over his shoulder and pulled her into his wide-open mouth. He grabbed her, holding her upright even though her body threatened to collapse. He licked her like she was a Popsicle, not just some damned little lollipop. He wanted her all in his mouth and he wouldn't stop until she was either dripping down his chin or begging for something else.

He was her plaything, and they were both going to love every second of it.

Her body moved in tandem with his tongue, rolling and pressing, pulling and sucking. It could have been minutes or hours, he had no idea. He was lost in her.

"Grant…" She moaned his name as he felt her clench around his tongue and gasp. "Oh my…" She moved, and he didn't miss a beat as she fell back against the wall and gave herself fully to her release.

She panted his name as she pulled him up to his feet. "You…are fantastic," she whispered, taking his lips and licking herself from them.

Reaching down, she slipped him inside her, and as she did, he knew that without a single doubt, he had found the woman and the place that could be his forever.

Chapter Fourteen

She was shocked Zoey hadn't texted or come and knocked on her door by now; she was normally super quick at pulling information from a multitude of sources even when on her own. Elle looked down at her watch. It was getting late.

The last thing Elle wanted to do was to move from her place on Grant's chest to pick up her phone and send Zoey a text, but now that she could think about something other than him, she needed to refocus on their case.

Lily was still missing, and Elle had to believe she was alive somewhere, just waiting for them to find her. Maybe Zoey had come up with something by now.

With a groan, she moved off his chest, and he finally looked up. "Where are you going?" he asked, touching her back as she sat up.

"Have you heard from anyone?" she asked, nudging her chin in the direction of his phone that was hanging haphazardly out of the back pocket of his pants. "I can't believe we actually got to be alone for this long. Normally one of our phones is going off." She frowned. Was something happening, something that was keeping everyone so busy that they had forgotten to inform them? Her anxiety rose.

He sat up, grabbing his phone as she did the same. "All I have is the regular thing—texts from my guys at the department and a few emails. Nothing to do with the case. You?"

She picked up her phone, and it vibrated in her hand. There was a text from Zoey.

Shit. What did we miss?

If something had happened while they had been making love and their temporary reprieve from reality had affected their case and finding Lily, she wasn't sure she would forgive herself—even though the sex with Grant had been absolutely breathtaking.

Zoey's text was vague, nothing more than Give me a call.

Did that mean she had found nothing? That all the information they had given her had proven to be of little use and they were really going to be starting from square one once again?

They shouldn't have waited. They shouldn't have taken any downtime. Why did the needs of their bodies, to feel one another, have to be so extreme?

She glanced over at Grant, who was leaning back in the bed and had one hand under his head against the headboard. His tattoo was stretched over his pec and she found herself staring at him again, wondering how she had gotten so lucky to find him in her bed.

If she wasn't careful, and if she didn't have such a personal connection to the case at hand, she could have easily found herself falling back into those arms and going for several more rounds. She could have made love to him every day for the rest of her life, if the fates would allow.

Yet she couldn't help but worry that now he had been with her, he was going to wake up from whatever lust trance she had managed to cast on him and realize he was out of her league.

She was an empowered woman in a male-dominated field, and logically she knew that what she felt was nonsensical, but she couldn't help the dark voice in the back of her mind that told her she wasn't enough for Grant. Unfortunately, this wasn't the first time she had felt this way around a man. The last time, she had tried to make the guy happy, telling him what he wanted to hear at the expense of being herself and living her truth. In the end, she had morphed into someone she had thought he wanted instead of her authentic self, the one he had said he had once loved.

She couldn't overthink this if she wanted to keep Grant. Well, if he wanted to keep her.

Running her hands over her face, she tried to wipe away the thoughts that were haunting her. She stood up and put on her clothes, slipping her phone into her pocket. She was almost afraid to face Grant in the event he would see she was already starting to feel insecure.

Though she was sure she could feel safe with him, and as soon as he pulled her back into his arms she would feel right at home, she feared it. To fall in love, to be her authentic self with this man was to make herself truly vulnerable. And any time she had ever been vulnerable with a man—well, with anyone, really—she ended up hurting.

Until she was sure he was worth suffering for, completely, she needed to protect her heart. And she wouldn't protect it by giving herself to him again, or by giving away any more of her power in what relationship they did have.

"I'll take by you getting dressed that Zoey must have texted you?" he asked, making her realize she had never really answered his ques-

tion and had just had an entire fight with him
without ever saying a word.

Or was it a fight? Maybe it was just her being
self-conscious.

If he took her in his arms and kissed away
all the feelings she was having right now, he
was the one—the man she could love, the man
who could read her body and just solve all of
her problems.

"She wants to see us." He picked up his
clothes and started to get dressed, too.

She'd hoped for a sign, maybe something
in neon, that suggested they had a future together—she would have liked for him to be her
forever—but she shrugged off the sentiment.
She wasn't a teen crushing on her idol. There
was work to do.

Making her way out to the kitchen, she grabbed
a bottle of water and a second one for Grant, putting his on the counter while she waited.

Hoping for a sign might have been too much
to ask for, but there had to be something that
told her he was the one…something he did or
said that could prove he wanted her for something besides her body and that thing that had
happened between them hadn't occurred just because it had been a possibility. She just needed
some kind of solid proof that this was *real* and

not just another lover—as much for herself as for him.

Her phone rang, and she pulled it from her pocket. It was Zoey. "Hello?"

She was met with the muffled sound of a phone being moved around and Zoey yelling things in the background. Though she wasn't sure what she was listening to, Zoey's voice made her blood run cold as she screamed for help.

The line went dead.

"Grant!" She dropped her water bottle.

He came running down the hall, his shoes untied. "What? Are you okay?"

"We have to go." She grabbed her coat and slipped her gun into her waistband as she moved outside.

He followed behind her as he readjusted his utility belt. "What's going on?"

"Zoey needs us." She motioned her chin in the direction of the office.

He tied his shoe and quickly caught up to her as she sprinted toward headquarters. There weren't any cars she didn't recognize in the ranch's parking lot, but that didn't mean anything. This ranch had been infiltrated by enemies before. It had happened before she was hired, but there was still talk about it to this day—normally after a night centered around campfires and whiskey, like the former attacks were some kind of horror story that were used to scare them at night.

It worked.

She shoved open the door to the office, and it slammed against the wall behind it. She expected to find Zoey midswing in some kind of fistfight. Instead, Daisy was on the ground wrestling with a stray dog Elle didn't recognize. The stray was bloodied and its ear was half hanging on, and as it jumped up to its feet, it snarled at her as though it was going to attack.

"Daisy!" Elle screamed, watching as her dog lunged, taking down the dark brown mutt-looking dog.

She wasn't upset with her dog, but she was afraid. Daisy was her baby. Nothing could happen to her baby. And yet, there was nothing she could do.

The dogs tore at each other, ripping with the teeth and diving for each other's throats. Daisy seemed to be winning, standing over the dog and having it pinned down to the ground between her front legs. But the brown dog broke free and grabbed Daisy's front leg and swept it out from underneath her, dropping her to the ground and taking the top.

Elle's throat threatened to close as she watched

the dog tear away at Daisy's fur, throwing black hair every which way around the office.

She looked up at Zoey, who was standing there, looking as at a loss as Elle felt. What had happened that had caused the fight? Then, what did it matter? All that mattered was that Daisy came away from this unharmed. She couldn't stand the thought of losing her baby.

Just like everything else that had gone wrong, this was her fault, too. She had been so stupid. She should have been focusing on her case instead of taking Grant to her bed. If she had just kept her head in her work, Daisy wouldn't have found herself in the position she was.

It was no wonder Elle couldn't keep Lily safe when she couldn't even keep her own dog from being hurt.

What would have ever possessed Zoey or the Clarks to ever entrust her with a damned child?

"Daisy, come!" she yelled, hoping the dog could hear her over the melee, but Daisy only looked at her with the white-eyed stress eyes of a dog in trouble.

She had to do something. There was no way she could stand here any longer and just watch as her dog was hurt.

Picking up an office chair, she jabbed at the snarling stray, pressing against it with the wheels until the dog unlatched from Daisy's throat. Elle's fingers pressed into the coarse carpet-like fabric as she lunged, using the chair like it was a door-breaching ram.

"Get out of here, dog!" she screamed.

Grant held open the door as she pushed at it with the chair until the brown dog stepped outside, its hackles raised and its teeth bared. When it realized it was no longer cornered in the office and had found its way back outside, the dog looked around wildly and took off in the direction of the mountains.

"What happened? How'd the fight start?" She turned on Zoey.

Zoey shook her head. "I think Daisy was trying to defend me, but I don't know. The dog just showed up and there was a snarl and…" She trailed off.

Daisy laid her head down on the ground and whimpered, and Elle ran over, sliding on her knees on the tile floor as she neared the animal. "Are you okay, baby? Mama is here," she said, careful to reach down and touch the dog gently in case she was still scared.

Daisy looked up at her with a sad, pained expression. "Let me look you over, honey. I promise I won't hurt you. I just need to check that everything is okay."

She looked back over her shoulder at Grant as she touched Daisy's shoulder. "You need to go find the other dog. Make sure it's okay. And it'll have to be tested for rabies."

He nodded, but he didn't look nearly as worried or upset as she did, and the thought irritated her. "And hurry about it. If that dog is hurt and heading to the mountains, we may never find it again if you don't move fast. I don't want to have any other lives on my hands." She spat the words, feeling the hurt in them but not allowing it to register.

Though she wasn't looking, she could feel the unspoken conversation that was happening between Zoey and Grant right over her head, and it pissed her off even more. She had every right to be angry—at the situation, at her choices and at the fact she had once again fallen short.

She was so goddamned tired of not being enough and of doing something for herself for once and instantly having to pay the price in a pound of her best friend's flesh.

She leaned into Daisy and put her forehead against the dog. "I'm so sorry, honey. I've got you, Daisy. I shouldn't have left you outside. I'm so, so sorry."

The dog leaned in and gave her a sweet lick to the side of the face, like she was accepting the apology, even though Elle was nowhere near deserving of the dog's mercy.

That, this bond between her and Daisy, was

what true love was. Pain and misery, injury and assault, and then forgiveness and love beyond all that agony. It was seeing a being at its worst and in its most vulnerable state and yet staying by their side.

It was endless faithfulness. No matter what.

No man, not even Grant, could offer her the same love as Daisy.

She had been a fool to be so selfish. Never again.

There was a growing pool of blood around Daisy's neck and chest. It stained the white tile floor, and Elle tried not to panic. Ever so gently, she ran her hands down the dog's body over the lumps and welts caused by the dog's bites and then around her thoracic area until her fingers felt the warm, wet tear just below her throat and at the front edge of her right shoulder.

"Baby…" she cooed, tears welling in her eyes and forcing her to blink them back. "Zoey, grab me some towels."

Zoey ran past her and headed toward the bathroom, coming out with a stack of hand towels and a roll of pink vet wrap. "Will this work?" she asked, handing it all over to her.

"Just press that towel right here, keep your pressure." Elle stood up and ran toward the back room where they kept all of their tactical gear in case they needed to bug out.

She pulled open her locker, exposing her black tactical bag, and pulled out a QuikClot kit she kept in it all the time in case of emergencies. She didn't know if the clotting agents would work on her dog, but she couldn't think of a reason they wouldn't. And, at the very least, it would slow the bleeding enough that she could hopefully get Daisy to the vet's office.

Elle made her way out to the main office and ripped open the kit. Zoey moved back, and she pressed the pad to the dog's exposed muscle. Daisy whimpered, trying to lick at the wound and pull off the gauze, but Elle kept her from getting to the pad. "Hold the pad there for a second," she said, motioning for Zoey to take over.

"It's going to be okay," she said to Daisy, repeating it over and over while she made sure the dressing stayed on the wound by wrapping it in the pink vet wrap.

From the look of the wound, it wasn't too bad as long as they got the bleeding stopped. After that, she would just need stitches and time to heal. Hopefully.

Elle pulled a shirt off the hook by the door and slipped it over the dog's head and covered up the wound and the dressing. "That's my good dog, Daisy. Mama has got you."

She stood up and, lifting with her knees, picked the rottweiler up. She held her against her chest as she looked over at Zoey. "Grab the door, will you?"

Zoey rushed by, holding open the office door and then jogging ahead of Elle to open up the back door of one of the ranch trucks. She put down a blanket and then helped lift Daisy inside. The dog's eyes were still wide, but now it appeared as if it was more the pain and most of the adrenaline had started to wear off.

Zoey ran back to the office and quickly locked up; when she came back, she was carrying the truck's keys.

Daisy let out a long, breathy moan and laid her head down on the blanket and gave Elle one more look before closing her eyes. The look made Elle's stomach pitch. Daisy was going to be all right. She had made her pup a promise, a promise she intended on keeping no matter what.

Clicking the back door shut gently, she made her way around to the passenger's side of the truck and moved to get inside. She looked toward the mountain, and as she did, she caught a movement out of the corner of her eye. Walking out of the woods, carrying the brown dog, was Grant. He'd wrapped the dog in a blanket, but it was looking up at him like he was some kind of hero.

She ran toward his truck and flung open the doors as he approached, carrying the other pup. Though she was upset about what had happened, it was terrible to ever see an animal in distress. "Is she okay?" Elle asked, motioning toward the dog as Grant moved to set her in the back.

"She is banged up, needs a few stitches. How's Daisy?" He ran his hand down the dog's head and scratched her gently behind the ears. The dog was panting but otherwise seemed to have fared better.

"Same, but seems to be hurting." She looked back over at Zoey. "We are heading to the vet's office. Follow us over." She started to jog back to the ranch truck but stopped and looked back at Grant. Her heart pulled her back to him, but if forced to choose, she couldn't leave Daisy alone. Not again.

"Grant?" she called, and he looked in her direction. "Thank you. I appreciate you finding the dog. You're a good man." She gave him a sweet, delicate smile and a tip of the head.

It had been a long time since she'd been around a man who wasn't on the Shadow team who could actually be trusted. It hurt her deeply to turn away from him and go to the ranch truck, to her waiting boss and her dog, but she knew she had to focus on the sure things in her life, and they included Daisy, Zoey and the STEALTH team. When she allowed herself to get distracted, she let them all down.

Chapter Fifteen

With the dogs back in surgery at the after-hours emergency vet clinic, Grant was left standing in the waiting room with Zoey and Elle. He had a sinking feeling that Elle felt this was partially his fault, that if they had been focusing on the things they had been hired to focus on, that none of this would have happened to her dog. He couldn't blame her.

Though he didn't own an animal, he understood the bond that came with owning one. He and his dog Duke had been inseparable until Grant had gone off to college. Duke crossed the rainbow bridge when he was away, and when he'd come home, it had never again felt the same. A part of him had gone over that bridge with his best friend.

If Elle was feeling even a small percentage of that same kind of pain, it was crazy to him that she was even allowing him to stand in the same room with her. The lady at the desk disappeared into the back, and Zoey finally turned to them. "This is probably going to take a while."

Elle nodded, and as he looked at her, he noticed how tired she looked. It wasn't just the kind of tired that was in the eyes. Instead, it appeared as though it was all the way down in her bones. He wanted to hold her and comfort her, but here in front of her boss seemed like one hell of a piss-poor place. She needed to keep it together in front of her boss, at least as much as she could, given the circumstances, and if he pulled her into his embrace, he had a feeling he would have to take her back to bed and hold her until her tears ran dry.

"I know you don't want to leave Daisy," Zoey said, looking down at her hands and then flipping her purple hair back and out of her face. "Did you ever get my text?"

Elle nodded.

"Did you manage to pull something?" Grant asked, hoping for the best.

Zoey pushed her hands over her chest and looked around as though making sure that they were alone and couldn't be overheard. "I had a phone call. It wasn't *great*."

His heart rate spiked. "What is that supposed to mean?"

Zoey looked over at Elle and then at him. "Senator Clark called me not long after you left my office." She cleared her throat like trying to remove the discomfort that was reverberating between them. "He made it clear that he will be pursuing a lawsuit against our group for negligence in the death of his wife and disappearance of his daughter. He is going to try and ruin us."

Holy shit.

Elle opened her mouth then closed it several times, and a single tear slowly escaped her eye and trembled down her cheek. "I… I'm so sorry." Elle sounded choked, like Zoey's statement was gripping her throat and threatening to kill the last parts of her soul that had, up until now, remained unscathed.

This was all his doing. Clark hadn't been gunning for Elle until they had pulled him off the woman admirer outside the airport. He should have known better than to publicly embarrass the senator, especially in front of a woman he might have been trying to get into his bed. The man was a narcissist, and while Grant was sure that he was hurting after his wife's death and the loss of his daughter, for a man like the senator, the worst kind of pain was always going to be the pain to his ego. He was nothing if he wasn't being pedestaled and revered—especially by the opposite sex.

"He is just looking for someone to blame," Grant said.

Elle looked at him, and there were more tears in her eyes. He could tell there were a million things she wanted to say, but in her current broken state he would take this on for her. If this was the only way he could show how much he cared about her, how much he secretly *loved* her, he was going to protect her. He was her man, even if only in his heart and only until the end of this case. She needed him, though she would never say it aloud.

"I know you're right," Zoey said, careful to avert her gaze from Elle in what he assumed was an attempt to allow Elle a moment to collect herself and keep her dignity intact.

He always hated losing his edge in front of a superior officer. That kind of thing had the power to kill a career, or at least throw a major hurdle in front of advancement. Maybe it was different for women, he didn't know, but he didn't think it would be good for her, either.

He stepped in front of Elle, shielding her with his body even though he was sure that Zoey cared for her. There was a bond between the two women, he could see it in the way they treated one another. No doubt, it was a saving grace in their line of work. It probably even provided them with some additional level of protection, to have a fellow woman at her side, but that didn't mean that weakness would be perceived as anything other than just that. And in teams like theirs, weaknesses could bring harm.

Elle exhaled, and he could feel her move behind him like she was brushing the tear from her face and shaking off the display of emotions. She stepped out and took her place beside him. "So, if you know it is just misplaced anger and this really isn't my fault—"

Zoey stopped her with a raise of her hand. "Whoa. I didn't say it wasn't our fault."

"You mean *my* fault," Elle said.

Zoey looked away. "All I'm saying is that things could have gone differently. There were definitely some aspects of our handling of our security duties that could have been better. Perhaps better communication from both sides of the desk would have stopped this from ever happening. Regardless, we are going to walk away from this incident with a large black eye and an even larger hit to our bankroll."

"Don't worry about your bankroll," Grant said. "I'm sure that we will make things right here. We will get Lily back and find whoever was responsible for Catherine's death."

"Even if you do, I don't know if that is going to stop the senator from gunning for us," Zoey said. "And as such, I can only do one thing to protect our company. It's something I don't want to do, Elle. Especially not here and now, but my hands are tied…at least until and *if* you guys can get the senator off our ass. Elle, I need you off the team."

Elle nodded. He expected her to cry, but instead her jaw was set and anger sparked in her eyes. She pushed past Zoey and made her way outside.

"What in the hell, Zoey?" he growled. "You don't move against your team members when they need you the most. She did her goddamned job, she did exactly what she was told and now you are taking this out on her? You are wrong right now in how you are handling this, and I think you know it. She was already hurting, and you just took her out at the knees."

Zoey started to say something, but he didn't want to hear it.

"I have been a part of this investigation from day one, and let me tell you, from everything I can see, she isn't the one in STEALTH who was the problem." He looked her up and down and then, without waiting for her to speak, he charged out of the office.

Elle was sitting in his pickup staring out through the passenger-side window and into space. He had no idea how he was going to fix this. Even if he could, he wasn't sure that the damage to her career would be repairable.

While STEALTH would likely recover, it was doubtful that Elle could say the same.

He still just couldn't believe that Zoey would have moved against one of her own like this, but going against a senator could be deadly if she and her team weren't careful. It was one of those situations in which it was live by the sword, die by the sword. They had chosen to work with vipers, now they would have to take the teeth.

Unfortunately, the teeth had pierced the neck of the mother of the child she had promised to protect.

As he got in and they hit the road, there was an impenetrable silence between them. He didn't know if he should tell her he was sorry or unleash a diatribe about how stupid her boss was, so he remained quiet. She and Zoey had been friends, but that probably only made what had just happened that much worse. She had been wounded by someone she trusted.

Her phone pinged, and he looked over and saw a text from Zoey flash over the screen. "What does she want?" he asked.

"I'm sure it's not to apologize and beg me to come back. And even if it was..." Elle sighed as she clicked the message off without reading it.

Grant touched her knee. "If you don't like your job, if you want to follow another path in life, you have my support. I will do whatever you need to help you out."

She chuffed. "I have no idea what to do right now. I don't have any damned answers. If you didn't notice, my entire life just came crashing down. The last thing I want or need is some guy who is only going to make things worse."

Was that what he had become, just *some guy*?

He wanted to argue with her, to tell her what she had just done to him and to his feelings. He wanted to tell her how all he wanted to do was be the man she needed and not like the men in her past who must have let her down. He loved her. But she mustn't have felt the same way.

In that case, he just needed to button his feelings up and cinch them down. He wasn't a fan of self-inflicted pain, and that's what he'd be doing to himself if he kept after her when it was clear she was dismissing him.

Though he was more than aware she was likely striking at him out of her own pain, he hadn't been prepared.

Yet, what did it matter? He had his answer as to her feelings toward him one way or another. At least it was a solid, unwavering rejection. A clear rejection was far better than half-assed feelings and empty promises.

"Stop," Elle said, touching his hand on her

knee as she stared down at her phone. "Pull over."

"What?" he said, jerking the wheel to the right and pulling the truck to the side of the road. "Are you okay?" he asked, forgetting he was hurt and angry at the mere thought that she needed him.

"I'm okay," she said, not really paying his question any mind. "Zoey said that she just managed to find another phone that was linked to the Clarks. She sent me the phone number, but said she is going to have her people dig into it, as well. Hoping to get the phone records as soon as she can."

He smiled; information like that was right in his wheelhouse. Opening up the computer that sat atop the truck's middle-seat console, he started it up. "What's the number?"

She rattled it off as he typed it into NexTx, a cellular tracking program used by law enforcement. He laughed wildly as the phone pinged. "You are going to love this," he said, turning the computer for her to see it.

"What am I looking at?"

"Right now, the phone is located near the Blackfoot River, just down I-90. Twenty minutes ago, it was moving. And five hours before that, it was in Mineral County."

"So what?" She frowned. "There is nothing

tying it to our case other than the fact it is a phone on the Clarks' account. For all we know, they had given one of their other employees a work phone."

He couldn't deny that she might be right. There were any number of reasons a senator and his wife would have needed a phone, but that didn't squash the feeling in his stomach that they had just stumbled on something; whether it would prove to be helpful or hurtful was up to time to tell, but at least it brought them something they needed most—hope in the time of darkness.

Chapter Sixteen

Elle looked down at her phone, half hoping that Zoey would send her another text and tell her that she was sorry, but she knew that it would never come. Even if Zoey was wrong, she wasn't the kind to apologize—ever.

Unlike her, Zoey was unflappable. She could stare into the fire and let the world burn down around her without ever blinking, even if she wasn't the one who threw the match.

Though she was incredibly angry, she couldn't hold a grudge against Zoey. Her boss had taken her on and allowed her to pursue her passion for K-9 work without even the tiniest of pressure to rush her dog's training. If anything, Zoey had been incredibly understanding about the kind of work she did and the benefit it was for the team. The only real mistake Zoey had made was allowing her to be assigned to the care of a senator's child.

It was Elle's failure that had brought them

here; Zoey was right. And she had been justi-
fied, actually *forced*, into letting her go. If Elle
had been thrust into Zoey's position, she probably would have made the same choice.

The road zipped by them as they drove down
the interstate in the direction of the Blackfoot
River, where Grant had gotten the ping on the
phone. He kept looking over at the computer,
checking to make sure that the phone's location
was relatively unchanging.

She couldn't believe his reaction to this minor
piece of evidence. It was like he saw this as their
saving grace, when there was no saving anyone
here. Her career was over, her dog was hurt and
they were on the rocks. And Lily was still missing. If this wasn't a last-ditch effort on his part
to save… *Wait, what is he trying to save?*

She glanced over at him, and there were
storm clouds in his green eyes. His brow was
furrowed, and even without reading his mind,
she could tell that he was on a mission. In a
strange way, it lightened some of the heavi-
ness in her heart. Her life had unraveled into
one huge heaping mess, one she couldn't bring
another person into out of the knowledge she
would never be able to give them everything
they deserved, but to know he was trying to
help her took some of the pain away.

There was nothing he could do to make it

all better, or take back what had happened to Daisy, but he was doing *something*. That said something about him. She had lost count of the people in her life who had made her promises only to find out they were as empty as the hearts of the people who had made them.

He was different, she could give him that. And, if her heart would have been capable, she could have loved him for it—maybe in another life.

Grant put his hand out, palm up, like he wanted her to reach over and take it. Though she wanted to, it would mean things she wasn't sure she wanted to promise. She was hurt, angry and emotionally compromised right now. And hadn't he been the one to tell her that was enough of a reason—being emotionally compromised, that was—not to get involved?

She pretended not to notice his extended hand, like it wasn't some kind of elephant in the pickup. Her fingers twitched like they wanted to come over and take his even without her mind agreeing to the plan. While she held no doubts about wanting him, he was just her type—hot, dominant, strong, and she'd be lying if she didn't say she loved how he protected her.

She liked to think she was tough, as she was more than capable of getting herself out of physically perilous situations, but when it came to the emotional ones, sometimes it was damn hard to be a woman.

"Elle." He said her name like it was a secret on his tongue, and the sound made her skin spark with yearning.

"Hmm," she said, trying to still seem the tiniest bit aloof.

"It's okay for you to hold my hand."

She looked over at him, and warmth rose into her face. Why did she always have that reaction when it came to him? She'd never thought of herself as much of a blusher, but when he talked to her like that and in that tone of voice, she melted.

"I…" she started, but she didn't know exactly how to express to him everything that she was feeling. "I… I don't want to be hurt anymore, Grant."

"No matter what happens, with any of it, I will keep you as safe as I can. I won't promise that you won't get hurt in this life, but I can promise you that I will do everything in my power to make sure that I'm not the one doing the hurting."

He didn't move his hand, and she stared down at his fingers. She wanted to believe him and give herself over to his beautiful words, but there was so much pain in her heart.

She sighed, and her hands trembled in her lap.

After a moment, she reached over and slipped her fingers between his. He couldn't take away the pain and guilt she was feeling, but at least she could have one positive thing in her life. And maybe doing this wasn't the smartest thing, getting involved when she wasn't at her best, but if she waited for a *right time*—a time that she was completely ready and at ease—she damned well could have been waiting forever. Her emotions and her life were always in flux. That was what life was, one fight rolling in on the shirt-tails of the one before.

She deserved something good in her life, and she would figure out how to do this love thing right—that was, if this was going to be a serious thing between them.

Did she ask him? Did he ask her for monogamy? She hadn't had a real boyfriend in so long that she couldn't quite remember how things had been made official with her last. In fact, maybe they hadn't been official—he'd been more than happy to step out of their relationship to sate some needs he later told her she hadn't been filling.

Why did she have to think about that right now? When things were starting to turn and go right? She needed to focus on Grant. Only on Grant. And just like earlier, she needed to be here with him. Beautiful, sexy things happened when she gave herself to him.

The thought of him between her legs made her shift in her seat. If she closed her eyes, she could still feel the last place his mouth had been on her. If only she could keep that feeling forever. But maybe that was just the afterglow speaking, all of this…the confusion and the weird feeling that was entirely too close to love. Love was perilous, at best.

But damn it if she didn't think she loved him. There was just something about being close to him. She loved to watch his mouth form words and the way his green eyes brightened when he spoke about things he enjoyed or memories from his past.

His thumb fluttered over her skin, and she closed her eyes for a moment, just taking in the full sensation that was his touch. Even her hand fit perfectly in his; how was that possible?

They got off the interstate and took a frontage road in the direction of the last ping off the phone. According to the tracking program, the phone was stationary and hadn't moved for the last thirty minutes.

"What are we going to do after this? Do you think we can pull anything else from the flight records? Maybe we should go see Steve again."

She tried to swallow back the anxiety that was rising within her.

He squeezed her hand, the simple action more effective to control her anxiety than anything she could have done. "If this doesn't pan out to be anything, don't worry. We will get Lily back. And, I told you…as for your job… you have plenty of options. If you can't stay at the ranch, I will help you find an apartment or whatever. You don't have to leave Montana."

She hadn't even thought about all the ramifications of losing her job with STEALTH yet. Of course, she couldn't stay at the ranch—that was headquarters for a group she no longer worked with. Zoey hadn't mentioned anything, but she had been trying to let her down gently—which was somewhat out of character for her. Zoey was far more the kind to have a spreadsheet and an exit survey to give people upon their firing.

She had been fired.

Her breath stuck in her chest, and her hands started shaking. She had no job, her dog was possibly going to have long-term damage regardless of what the vet said and now she couldn't breathe.

Grant glanced over at her and frowned as he looked at her complexion. "Babe, take a breath. In. Out. In and out." He breathed a few times like the problem was that she had forgotten how,

not that her body was trembling on the preci-
pice of a full anxiety attack.

"Don't freak out." He paused his breathing exercise. "What can I do to help you?" He
started to pull the truck over, but she waved
him off.

"No," she said, trying to mimic the Lamaze-
style breathing. "Don't stop."

He smiled at her like he was deciding whether
or not to say what was just on the tip of his
tongue.

"What?" She inhaled.

"The last time you said *don't stop* was at your
cabin," he said, giggling as he blushed. It was
crazy to see him act in a way she had been chas-
tising herself for, and him looking absolutely
sexy while doing it.

A giggle escaped her as she exhaled. It felt
strange, like with the giggle she was finding
her center again.

He laughed harder, but she didn't know if
it was at her or the situation or what, and she
began laughing harder, too. She laughed until
tears started to form at the corners of her eyes.
It didn't make sense and maybe this was some
kind of mania or magic, but she could feel the
craziness that had overwhelmed her seep out
with every laugh. Her heart lightened as her
tears fell. Maybe this laughter was the catharsis

her soul needed, especially since it was brought on by and hand in hand with Grant.

He was changing her life. He was willing to pick her up when she was at her lowest. He hadn't said he cared, but he had to have cared for her. Maybe he couldn't make all of her problems disappear, but he could damned well make things lighter.

The computer flashed, and Grant pulled his hand away so he could navigate the screen while also driving. "The phone is here," he said, looking around like there would be some kind of sign pointing directly to the device.

She let her giggles go dry and ran her hands over her face, wiping away the remnants of stress. Her life would be okay. She had a friend, even more than a friend, in Grant. She could see things lasting for a long time if they would make whatever it was they were doing official, but even if they remained only between-the-sheets friends, then she would have to be satisfied.

Until the future came, all she had to do was help the little girl who needed her the most. She wouldn't give up on her, no matter what.

Grant pulled the pickup onto the side road where the program had dropped the last ping for the phone's location. The road was a fishing access point, and there were several brown-and-white signs marking the spot, one with a draw-

ing of a fish on a line, another with the image
of a boat. She'd driven by many of these signs
while in Montana, but she couldn't say that she
had ever actually driven into one before. They
came to a stop at a large roundabout parking
area with a boat launch.

The river was flowing, but ice pocked the
edges and a white mini-berg floated past them.
It was odd to think anything the senator owned
would be at a place like this.

Elle picked up her phone. "I need to know
if Zoey managed to get the phone records for
the number. And check to see if she found anything on Philip." She tapped the message and
hit Send, not listening to the voices in her head
that told her she had no business reaching out to
her ex-boss. Zoey would help them if she could;
they were friends.

As she waited for a reply, Elle gazed around
the parking area. There were a few trucks
parked tailgate into the spot in true Montana
man style. What was it about men here that
made them all want to prove to the world how
good they were at driving a truck? Her smile
returned.

In the farthest corner of the lot, away from
all the trucks, was a crossover. It was muddy,
and its wheel wells were caked in the muddy

brown ice brought on after hours of interstate driving in winter conditions.

"There," she said, pointing at the car.

"Good a place to start looking as any," he said, smiling over at her. "Good eye."

He parked next to the red Subaru, and she got out and walked over beside the car. There was no one inside, and from the lack of ice over the engine on the hood, it was clear it had been recently driven. Inside the car was a collection of fast-food wrappers, one from Sonic—a chain that didn't have restaurants anywhere close. Either the driver had been all over the west and had just gotten back, or they were terrible at cleaning up their mess.

She glanced at the car's license plates; it was from Montana and started with a four—the number for Missoula County. Snapping a picture, she texted the plate to Zoey, as well.

Grant turned away and started to type the license plate number into his computer in the truck.

She stepped around the back of the car. In the back seat was a small booster seat. Her heart jumped. Had Lily been in this seat?

She bit back the thought. There was nothing to indicate that this search for the phone actually had anything to do with Lily. If anything, it was just one more possible lead they had to work through only to be left empty-handed. Her hopes were running away with her reality.

"You're not going to believe this," Grant said. "That car is registered to one Philip Rubbick."

Her phone vibrated with a message from Zoey almost at the same time as Grant spoke. Looking at the message, Elle's mouth dropped open. "Zoey says Philip 'Ace' Crenshaw is the owner of NightGens LLC. He hid his ownership under a bunch of other names of businesses, so it was hard to find."

"The company that owned the helicopter?"

"One and the same." She lifted the phone in her hand so he could see the text Zoey had sent them.

He smiled, his eyes filled with hope and excitement. "That means that it's likely Philip 'Ace' Crenshaw and Philip Rubbick are one and the same—Steve's brother."

"Holy crap." Had they finally pieced the puzzle edges together? She put her arms on the windowsill of the truck as she tried to pull together and make sense of everything she and Grant had just learned. "If Steve was working for this other crew, why would he have said he worked with STEALTH?"

"Smart move on his part, really. He sent us on a dead lead. In the meantime, while we were chasing our tails, he got to talk to his brother and tell him that we were getting closer." Grant scratched at the stubble on his chin. "I can't believe I screwed it up. I even noticed the marks on Steve's hands."

"What?" she asked, frowning.

"When someone stabs another person, especially when enraged, they often cut and damage their own hands. And Steve…well, his hands were mangled. But, to be honest, they matched the rest of him. Like I said, he threw me off my game. I should have paid more attention," he grumbled.

"That's not your fault. Now that we have some answers, we will just get your people to go pick him up."

He wasn't done whipping himself. "I can't believe I never asked Steve if he knew Philip. It didn't even cross my mind that they would be related. I didn't go deep enough. Maybe if I had, we wouldn't have gone on a wild goose chase and Daisy wouldn't have gotten hurt."

"None of that was your doing." She put her hand on his arm, trying to return some of the comfort that he had brought her. "Besides, we did have some *fun* while we were waiting. I have to believe that everything happens for a reason. And we could have looked into a million things deeper and not found answers. Don't be so hard on yourself."

He put his hand on hers and intertwined their fingers. He leaned down and kissed her knuckles ever so gently. "First, I have a feeling that regardless of what would have happened, we would have had some *fun* together. It just wouldn't have been the same."

"Does that mean you still regret it?" She lifted a brow in warning that he should take a minute to think long and hard before answering.

He chuckled. "I regret nothing when it comes to you, and us." He turned her hand over and kissed her open palm. "From the ugliest moments, we can build beautiful futures."

She didn't move. Futures? Did that mean he thought this was going somewhere? They were going to be fly-by-night, or fly-by-the-case, lovers? She loved the thought.

"We…" She pulled her hand back and patted the windowsill. "We probably need to focus."

He looked slightly crestfallen, and she immediately felt guilty for her response.

"I mean, I'm glad you don't regret anything," she said, tilting her head and sending him a gentle smile. "I most certainly don't, because there is something between us. I don't know what it is, but there's something I've never felt before. It's like you and I *fit*."

The look of hurt left his eyes, and his smile returned. "I hope that's not just the kiss talking."

"What kiss?"

"This one," he said. Taking her face in both of his hands, he pulled them together.

She leaned into the cold steel of the dirty truck, not caring about the mud that would be all over her clothes or the way the cold, wet road grime was threatening to pull all the heat from her body. All she cared about was the way his tongue worked over the edge of her lip and flicked at the tip of her own. She pulled his lower lip into her mouth and gently sucked on it. She could never kiss this man enough. His lips were like sugar, addictive in all their sweetness.

He ran his thumbs over her face, gently caressing her skin as their kiss slowed. He leaned back, searching her eyes, and the look in his gaze made her heart shift in her chest—almost as if the entire beast had moved locations in her chest, forward and closer to him.

She took his hands in hers and, removing them from her face, she kissed his open palm. "You are incredible."

"And so are you," he said, his voice husky.

"Let's find this phone. Maybe it has something about Lily on it. Then we can focus on what we are going to do about us," she said, though right now she knew exactly what she wanted to do with him and his body.

"Yes," he said, rolling up the truck's window and turning off the ignition before getting out.

She took the moment to readjust the holster inside the waistband of her pants. She always hated sitting in a car with them, but at least her gun was small and could go unnoticed and unseen.

"You warm enough?" he asked, grabbing a pair of gloves from his door and slipping them on. "You need some gloves?" He motioned to the cubby in the door where another pair of large men's gloves rested.

"No, thanks," she said, aware that her hands would be freezing if they were outside for any long period of time. She stuffed her hands in her coat pockets. "Hopefully we will be moving enough to stay warm and we will make quick work of getting this phone into our custody."

She looked over at the car. "Do you think it's in there?" she asked, pointing at the window.

He shrugged. "If it is, there's nothing we can do without getting a warrant to do a search."

"Did you check the phone's location again? Does it tell you exactly where we can find it?"

He pinched his lips closed. "Unfortunately, it's not pinpoint accurate. That being said, it's going to be close. I'm thinking within five hundred yards of the pin, give or take some."

"Do you think you should call in some more deputies? Maybe they can help us look over the area?"

He took out his phone. "I'll text a couple of them. If they're not busy, they can join us."

She totally understood. "Maybe they're bored and would like to pursue a lead with us."

He laughed. "They might be. There weren't many open calls." He pointed toward his computer inside the pickup. He zipped up his jacket and pulled on his gloves. "On days like these, where there aren't a lot of calls, I used to look for things like this to do. There are times when I miss being on patrol instead of mostly sitting behind a desk and filling out reports, but I don't miss the slow days."

He reached down and took her hand in his.

"Right now, I could use some slower days." Their footfalls crunched in the snow.

"I hear you there, but for what it's worth, I'm glad all this brought me to you."

"I would have preferred different circumstances, maybe meeting you at a bar or something." She leaned into him, touching his arm as they followed the footsteps that led from the car and toward a hiking trail. The snow cover was patchy, with swaths that had thawed and refrozen and areas where the powder had completely receded and patches of cottonwood leaves littered the ground.

The single set of footprints that had led from the mess of footprints around the car soon disappeared and was consumed by the forest. Though they had a lead here, a solid lead to someone who very well could have known what happened to Catherine and Lily, something about the situation still felt strange, *off* in a way that Elle couldn't quite put her finger on.

They walked slowly, searching the edges of the trails for any signs of a discarded cell phone. If Steve had told Philip that they had gotten on their scents, it was more than possible that Philip had discarded the car and the cell phone at this access. It was doubtful that they were actually going to find Philip, but they would do the best they could with the information they had.

The world smelled of biting cold, tall drying sweet grasses, rotting leaf litter, all mixed into the swirling odor of clean river water. Walking around a gentle bend in the trail, they came to the river.

A man was sitting on the bank, his head down and his knees up. His arms were outstretched, palms together. He looked at odds with the world in only a black sweatshirt and jeans. She couldn't see his face, but there were touches of gray in the brunette hair at his temples. His neck had a long scratch on the back that was still bleeding.

"Hey," Grant said, calling out to the man.

The man jerked, and he looked up. His gaze moved from Grant to Elle. His eyes widened as Philip recognized her. "What in the hell are you doing here?"

Philip reached behind his back and moved his hand under his sweatshirt to a bulge that Elle knew all too well was a gun. She hoped she was wrong; she hoped she didn't have to do what she had been trained to do in a situation like this, but as he moved the cloth of his sweatshirt back, she saw the exposed black grip and the butt end of a Glock.

Her hand dropped to her own gun, and in one swift movement she cleared her shirt, drew the weapon, aimed and fired. It all happened fast. A single motion. As the round left the gun, she saw the spray of black gunpowder. She'd never noticed that before with this gun. Was it a dirty round? What kind of ammo had she been using? It was whatever STEALTH had provided. They wouldn't have used dirty rounds.

And then she realized she needed to come back to the moment. She couldn't stop shooting until the threat was completely neutralized.

When a person was shot, they didn't stop. Inertia and adrenaline could keep a person moving even if they received a fatal wound. Philip was proving to be the kind of target that she had trained for. She let her finger move forward on the trigger, letting it click to reset, and then she pulled slowly again. It was almost a surprise as the second round left the barrel. She wasn't sure where she had hit Philip, but she had been aiming at center mass. In training, she was normally never more than a few centimeters off at this kind of range.

She'd definitely hit him, but Philip pulled his gun. He took aim and she fired again, but as her finger pulled on the trigger, Grant rushed at her from her left and pushed her out of the way, his gun in hand. Shots rang out, but she wasn't entirely sure who had done the shooting.

Her Sig Sauer kicked out the hot brass, and it skittered beside her as her shoulder hit the ground.

Blood. There was so much blood.

Chapter Seventeen

The ground was red around Philip where blood seeped deeper into the snow, melting it and diluting the blood further. The man had dropped the gun in his hand when he had collapsed, his muscles going limp in death. The side of his face was pressed into the ground, and his hands were opened at his sides.

Elle was lying on her back in the snow, and he could make out the sounds of her erratic, amped breathing. He knew that feeling well thanks to the many fights he'd been in while working patrol. That adrenaline hit affected everything.

At her side was a patch of red blood. She'd been hit. He'd been too slow to help her.

It shouldn't have gone anything like this.

"Are you okay?" Grant asked. "Where does it hurt?"

She was running her hands over her body, as though even she wasn't sure where the bullet had torn through her. She had been hit—there was no question about the blood that was pooling around her.

He wished this had all played out differently. If he had been paying attention to what he should have been paying attention to, Elle would have never gotten hurt.

"Is he down?" She pointed in the direction of Philip.

Grant stepped over to him and pressed his fingers against his neck, searching for the pulse. He found nothing. "He's gone."

"That was not at all how I wanted that to go down," she said.

She moved to sit up, but as she did, he could tell the world swam around her and she was forced to lie back down in the snow. "I already called dispatch. The troops should be here soon. But it's a bit of a drive for EMS to get here, so we're going to have to keep you calm and your blood pressure low. I need to take care of that wound. Stop the bleeding." He pointed to her midsection. "Open your coat and lift up your shirt."

She moved to wave him off, but as she did, she grimaced in pain. Her adrenaline must have been starting to decrease and allowing the pain to set in. "I'm fine. Really," she said, though he already knew better.

"Do you have to be stubborn right now?"

"Do you always have to try and get me naked?" she teased, closing her eyes as she laughed.

He squatted down beside her and started to help unzip her jacket. The bullet had pierced through the jacket's shell and the goose down, red with blood, was poking out.

If only he had reacted quicker, he would have been the one to take the hit instead of her. At least she had been able to draw down on the target; she definitely moved faster than both him and the other man.

It was easy to see she had spent thousands of hours training for a moment like that. Hell, from her reaction alone, he doubted that this was her first time in a life-threatening situation. Later, he'd have to ask her about it.

No doubt, somewhere in her contracting past, there were literal skeletons. He didn't judge her for any of it, but he didn't envy her, either. Being in a situation like this, where a life was taken and more lives were still at risk, left long-term scars. And he didn't mean the scars that would be left by any physical wounds.

"I am going to open up your shirt. Is that okay?"

She nodded. "I think I'm okay. It hurts but I'm going to make it."

She was talking to him, which was a good sign, but he had to see the damage for himself.

He gently lifted up the hem of her shirt. On the left side of her abdomen was a dime-size hole. "I'm going to roll you slightly. Just tell me if I need to stop. Okay?"

She bit her lip but nodded.

As he moved her, he spotted a larger exit wound on her back where the bullet had passed through her body.

He was surprised, given the velocity in the range of the round, it hadn't hit him, as well. In a single shot, Philip could have had them both.

"The good news is it looks like it went straight through. Hopefully it didn't hit any major organs, but from where it's located, I think it's important that you don't move and we try to keep you as still as possible." He laid her back down, flat. Gently, he lowered her T-shirt and zipped her coat back up, trying to keep her as warm as he could.

"How did the bleeding look?"

"Actually, it looked pretty clean. The bleeding appears to just be oozing, but make sure to hold some pressure on the wound." He stood up.

"What are you doing?" she asked, putting her hands to her abdomen and pressing.

"I'm going to go grab my medical kit. I'll be right back. Don't move." There was a lump in his throat as he jogged back to his pickup and grabbed his red first aid kit. He could at least stop the bleeding and get her stabilized and ready for the EMS teams when they arrived.

Yet he couldn't help the nauseating feeling that he was the one who was responsible for all this happening. It had been his brilliant idea to come out to the middle of the woods, nowhere near emergency care, and then he'd ended up getting her shot.

If he had only reacted faster. Pulled the second he saw Philip's hand moving toward the gun. But he hadn't been completely sure that the man was going for a gun. They hadn't provoked him, but Grant should have known the shape under the man's sweatshirt. He'd seen it a million times before, but his hope had run away with his good sense.

He had promised himself and Elle that he would protect her, and now she was lying out there bleeding into the snow after having taken down a man. And for what? They hadn't found Lily, and Philip had pulled the trigger before they got any answers.

Her shooting had solidly been in self-defense and every jury would side with her, especially with him as her witness, but they would still have to sit through endless rounds of questioning and he would have to sit through IA questions and hearings before being cleared. This was going to take so much out of both of them, and all because he had chosen to go on a wild goose chase.

No. He had just been doing his job to the best of his abilities. He was making choices based on the information they had been able to accumulate up to this point. Sometimes bad things happened, and in this case, inexcusably terrible things, but there was no going back and fixing his mistakes. He couldn't focus on that right now; instead, he needed to focus on helping Elle in the only ways he could.

As he made his way back to Elle, he found she had moved and was now sitting up next to Philip. She was still gripping her side. In her hand was a black phone he didn't recognize. She was tapping away with one finger, and for a moment he wondered if that was in fact the cell phone they had been looking for. But if it was, how had she found it?

"Elle, why are you sitting up?" he asked, looking at her back where the blood had stained her jacket and was oozing freely from the hole.

She shook her head, ignoring his reprimand. "I found his phone."

"Philip's? Where?"

She shrugged as she looked back over her shoulder at him and gave him a guilty smile. "Well, it was ringing from his pocket."

"You and I both know you had no business

disturbing the crime scene," he said, walking over to her and opening up his first aid kit.

He hated to admit it, but if he had been in her shoes, he would have probably done the same damned thing—procedure or not.

"Business or not, I think you'd be interested to hear that it was Steve on the other end of the line."

He stopped and stared at her. "Did you answer it?"

She nodded. "The number came up as restricted, and when I answered the guy Steve started talking. He said something about Lily, and then, 'The senator changed his mind. He wants us to keep her safe.' When I didn't say anything, I think he got suspicious and he hung up."

"But you never spoke?" Grant asked, worried now that if Steve knew they were on the receiving end of that phone call, they could have found themselves in more danger than they were already in.

"No." She shook her head. "He didn't know I was there, I promise."

"But he must know something was up with Philip." His entire body clenched. "And if they were talking about the senator, they must be on his payroll. It's going to be hard to prove in court, if we ever get them there and get Lily back, but I think the senator may have a whole lot more to do with his wife's death than he alluded to."

"No kidding," she said, clicking on the phone screen, but it had locked.

Grant sat down beside her in the snow. "Here, let me get this QuikClot on you. I don't want you losing any more blood. I can't lose you."

She stopped working on the phone and looked over at him with a gaze he hadn't seen her give him before. He could have expected hate, disgust or even disappointment after the situation he had gotten them into and the pain he had caused her, but instead she looked at him with what appeared to be *love*. Those eyes—those beautiful almond-shaped blue eyes—when she gave him that look, he was surprised the snow around them didn't melt.

"Lift your shirt. Let me take care of you."

She put down the phone and pulled up her jacket and her shirt, exposing the exit wound as he slipped on a pair of gloves. He packed the wound and taped down the gauze, then moved around to her front and repeated the treatment. The entire time, he could feel her staring at him, but he wasn't sure why and he wasn't sure he wanted to ask. If he asked and the look in her eyes wasn't love, it would hurt. And he was already hurting because of the mistakes he had made when it came to her.

As he put down the last piece of tape, he finally looked up at her as he took off his nitrile gloves and slipped them into his pocket to throw away later.

"Grant," she said, her voice soft.

"Hmm?" His fingers moved over the tape one more time as if he was checking to make sure that it was firmly adhered, but in truth all he wanted to do was keep touching her. He needed to touch her skin, to know she was okay, to know she was going to make it through this.

"Thank you," she said, touching his face gently with her fingertips.

"No. I'm so, so sorry." His voice cracked with all his feelings, feelings he couldn't make heads or tails of right now. "This happened because of me. If I'd just gotten the drop on him first. Or if we hadn't walked up from behind him... Hell, maybe I should have just tried to take him down before he drew down on us. I screwed up, Elle, and you are hurt because of me."

She shook her head. "I don't care about a stupid bullet wound. I'm telling you now, I've seen things like this happen before—this kind of wound—and I will be all right. If anything, at least I will have a cool story to tell at the bars on a Friday night," she teased. "But really, this wasn't your fault. From day one, actually from the day I put my hand on my first pistol, I knew this could happen. I knew the risks. I made the choices."

"But I put you in front of the round that hit you."

"Technically, you did try to push me out of the way. If you hadn't, I would probably be in an entirely different situation right now. So, really, you saved my life." She ran her thumb over his cheek as she looked into his eyes. "I owe you my life, Grant."

He was left speechless. All he could do was touch her hand with his and kiss her open palm. He pressed his face into her palm.

"We need to focus, Grant. I can't have you feeling bad. Seriously, we need to focus on Lily. When we get back, we can focus on us."

Though she was making a good point, he didn't want to move out of her hand. He pulled back. "Yeah, Lily." He ran his hands through his hair and down over the back of his neck as he stood up and away from her.

"Do you think Philip did something to her?" She pointed to the scratch on Philip's neck. "Do you think that was why he was sitting here, by the river?" Her gaze moved to Philip's dead body and then out to the icy water.

A little girl couldn't survive water like that

even when it wasn't ice cold and whispering of hypothermia. Only a monster would have killed a little girl, but monsters were one thing he was used to dealing with—and though Elle had been strong through this shooting, if Lily was lying out on the riverbank somewhere, that could break anyone.

"I'm sure she's okay." Grant looked around like he would suddenly see the little girl just standing on the riverbank, silently watching them and grateful that they had finally found her. Yeah, right, like they could get that lucky.

He looked over at Philip's body. There had been a car seat in the Subaru. It was possible that Lily could have been around here, but maybe he had dropped her off with someone else—maybe Steve had told him to ditch her and run. There were any number of possible scenarios that could have played out before they came upon this man.

But maybe there was something on the body that could help them find the girl. Something, anything, was better than nothing at all—and though he hated the thought, they needed to have answers even if those answers meant Lily was dead.

Chapter Eighteen

Elle tried not to focus on the pain in her side. She had told Grant she was going to be fine, that she wasn't hurting too bad, but the pain threatened to burn through her like a hot iron. She'd heard it burned when a person had been shot, but she had never expected this kind of intensity. She could only imagine what it must feel like to have a baby; if it was anything like this, she would be adopting.

Parents didn't have to be blood relatives of a child. If Senator Clark had anything to do with his wife's death and his daughter's disappearance like they had come to assume, then it only proved the point that guidance and love determined parentage more than biology. She could provide those things to a kid. She wouldn't even adopt a baby—rather, she would adopt an older kiddo. She wanted to bring a child into her life that had no one, nowhere to go and had felt abandoned by the world.

If Lily was found safe and alive, she silently made a promise to the ether that she would follow through and adopt a kid someday. She would give them more love and guidance than even she had received. If she was hoping and praying to the ether, she added in a prayer for Daisy to be healthy, too.

She also added a plea for Grant to be hers. This time, thinking about him and their future didn't feel like such an outrageous dream.

Maybe it was too much to ask for it all, but she didn't care.

Picking up the black phone she'd taken from the dead man, she reached over for Philip's thumb so she could open up the device. However, as she moved to touch him, she noticed a tuft of hair. There, under his pointer and middle fingers, was a clump of fine blond hair. It was the same color as Lily's.

Her heart fluttered in her chest. What did that hair mean? "Grant," she said, "look." She pointed at Philip's hand. "That's Lily's hair."

"Are you sure?" Grant asked, moving beside the body and taking his phone out and snapping a picture of the hand holding the wispy blond locks.

The hair was dry. Did that mean she hadn't been in the water or that he had been holding the hair in his hand long enough for it to dry after he had committed murder?

"She has to be around here," Elle said, standing up. "We have to find her."

"Elle, you aren't in any kind of shape to go search for Lily. If she is out here, our team is on their way. We can start our search as soon as they get here."

She put her hand on the cottonwood tree next to her, steadying herself as she got up and on her feet. "And what if she is out there in the water somewhere? Wet and hurt? Do you think she can really wait? It's cold and she is likely alone. She has to be so scared."

He looked down at Philip and then back up at her. "If you promise not to go anywhere—"

"I'm not making any promises to that effect, Grant. So you can either help me look for her or you can get out of my way. We are so close to her. I have to find her. I have to know she is okay."

Grant shook his head. "I'm not going to let you put yourself in more danger. For all we know, you could be bleeding internally. You know I want to find Lily, too. Finding her has been the major driving force behind this entire case. But let's say she is deceased. You risking your life is not only dangerous, but it's downright illogical."

She knew he made sense and that his admonition was coming from a good place, but she wasn't about to sit here and do nothing when the child she loved more than herself was possibly hurt somewhere near. "I'm telling you, Grant, if she is out here and relatively unharmed, she is not going to answer or come near anyone she doesn't know or trust."

Grant ran his hands over his face in frustration, but he had to have known he wasn't going to get anywhere in this fight. There would be no stopping her, not now.

"You know kids. She is probably terrified right now. And they always make everything their fault. That means she likely feels everything that has happened to her up to this point is because of some mistake she made. What if she thinks she is going to get in trouble? Can you even begin to imagine how scared she is right now? She has been through so much." Her voice cracked. "I can't. I can't sit by and do nothing."

Grant sighed like he understood and empathized with what she was saying but still didn't agree.

She loved him for the way he wanted to protect her and keep her safe, but this wasn't about her. This was about someone else she loved, someone she had promised to protect and some-

one she had let down. This was about an innocent, sweet child.

"I know you want to do the right thing by everyone here. It's what makes you the man you
are—the good man, the man I have come to
love—but I have to find Lily." She paused. "If
only we had Daisy."

"How about I call in the other K-9 teams? We
can get them on this." He smiled. "And wait…
did you just say you *loved* me?"

She wasn't sure if the faintness she was feeling was because of her admission or because of
blood loss, but she found she needed to press
her shoulder against the tree so it could support more of her weight. She sent Grant a sexy
half smile. "Loving you is easy to do. You are
the perfect combination of all the things I have
been looking for in a partner. I never thought
I'd meet anyone like you, and then you just appeared in my life."

He blushed and looked away.

Shit. She hadn't meant to admit her love for
him. Not here. Not yet. And then there he was,
not saying it in return. He didn't love her. He
was going to run away.

She pushed herself off the tree, not giving
him another second to come up with something
to say instead of "I love you, too."

As she walked toward the river and away

from him, she wasn't sure what hurt worse, the bullet wound or the pain in having her love rebuffed.

"Elle, stop. Wait," he called from behind her.

Yeah, right. The last thing she wanted to do right now was look him in the eyes. She had just made a hard situation impossibly harder. And there was no reeling back in the words she had let fall from her lips. She couldn't believe her own stupidity.

She knew better.

She had always vowed to never tell a man she loved him before he told her. And there she went breaking her own rules for a man who didn't even feel the same way.

What an idiot.

If she wasn't going to die from her wound, she was certainly going to die from embarrassment. She started walking down the riverbank, downstream.

"Elle, please stop," he said, only steps behind her.

She shook her head, afraid that if she opened her mouth to speak, all the pain she was feeling would come spilling out and she would say more things that she would regret.

"Don't be like that, Elle. You just caught me off guard. I didn't expect you to—"

"Lily!" she yelled, cutting him off. She didn't

want to hear his excuses. There was only one acceptable response to someone telling a person they loved another. He started to make a sound. "Lily!" she called again.

If Elle could have run away, she would have, but her feet slipped on the icy river rocks and every step she made was deliberate to keep from sliding and falling. She didn't need Grant having to rescue her again.

Thankfully, the third time he tried to talk to her and she called out Lily's name, her adolescent stonewalling took effect and he stopped trying. She felt stupid for treating this situation—a situation she had caused—like this, but she couldn't think of another way to make things less awkward. It just was what it was at this point, and she had no one else to blame than herself. She had read the feelings between her and Grant incorrectly.

As they walked, the only sound became the gurgle and rushing sounds of the river, their footsteps clattering on the cobbles, and the occasional call of magpies and ravens in the distance. Her ego was definitely feeling more pain than her side, and it threatened to bring her to her knees.

It was fine, though. After they got through this investigation, she could go back to being by herself. She could find another job, and if nothing else she could train dogs at some chain store or something. The last thing she wanted to do was go back into contracting work, going overseas and watching as hellish crimes happened to the most innocent people. Though, admittedly, she didn't have to go overseas to find those kinds of monsters.

To her right, she heard the sounds of whimpering. The sound was soft and mewing, and Elle stopped walking in hopes it wasn't just in her imagination.

"Ms. Elle?" Lily's voice broke through the pain filling Elle's soul.

"Lily? Lily, is that you?" she called, her voice taking on a manic, relieved tone.

Tucked into the hollowed-out center of a cottonwood, barely visible in the distance, was Lily. She was wearing a dark blue coat and white boots, and she waved a dirt-covered gloved hand.

Tears sprang from Elle's eyes and poured down her cheeks as she forgot about her own pain and rushed toward the little girl. She stepped over downed trees and pushed through the brush, and as she grew closer Lily stood up and started to run toward her. Lily extended her arms, throwing them around Elle's legs as they found one another.

As she pulled her up and into her embrace, Elle wasn't sure who was crying harder or was more relieved.

Chapter Nineteen

The hospital staff had been incredibly kind in allowing Lily and Elle to stay together in the emergency room. In all reality, even if they had tried to pull them apart, Grant was sure that neither would have allowed it. Even during the ride in the ambulance, the two ladies had been inseparable, according to the EMS workers.

After Elle had told him she loved him, all he could think about was her, and if Lily hadn't called out to them, he was sure that he wouldn't have seen her hiding away in the tree. Elle had been right, and as much as he had hated the idea of her striking out into the woods to find the girl, it was because of her that Lily had been found.

He made his way toward their room and knocked on the door frame. Elle was lying down in the hospital bed, Lily's head on her chest. Lily's eyes were closed, and from the steady rise and fall of the little girl's back, he could tell she was fast asleep.

Elle looked up at him as he made his way inside. There was hurt in her eyes, but he doubted it had anything to do with her side. Whatever she had been feeling from that had likely been fixed with some kind of meds by now, which meant the pain in her eyes was one he had put there.

"How are you two doing?" he asked.

She nodded. "Lily is all good. They checked her out, and aside from a few bruises and a missing patch of hair, she seems to be not too worse for the wear. The only thing they want me to watch are her feet. Her little toes were pretty cut up after walking barefoot in the snow when Steve took her from the house."

"Is that what she said had happened?"

Elle nodded. "She won't tell me what happened with her mother, but I'm hoping it is because she didn't see her mother's death. I didn't press her too hard about details. I'm sure when she is feeling a little better, we can talk more, and I'm sure she'll be assigned a counselor. I just wanted her to feel safe and secure for now." Elle paused. "The hospital asked if they should contact the senator."

"What did you tell them?"

"She is a minor, and he is her parent. They

were put into a tough situation." She paused. "I told them we needed to wait to hear from you. You are in charge of this investigation."

"I appreciate that." He smiled, stepping closer to her and putting his hands on the rail of her bed. "I think we can make that work. I'll call my teams in and we can arrest the senator in the parking lot—away from Lily. They have already taken Steve into custody. He didn't put up a fight, and he has been happy to talk."

"That's surprising." She chuckled gently, as though she wanted to keep her movement to a minimum in order to not disturb the sleeping child.

"Yeah," Grant said, smiling. "The only thing he was worried about was the stupid goat. He made sure that it was taken to the neighbor's house before he left. Sounds like he is going to give up everything—including the senator. He already told my team all about the senator hiring him and his brother—and how the senator was going to try and pin everything on them thanks to the falsified death threats."

"No doubt the senator has lawyered up by now," Elle said, rolling her eyes.

He felt exactly the same way. "I'm sure he has."

"Did Steve tell your team why the senator

hired them? Was it his intention to kill the girls?" Elle whispered.

"I think he wanted his wife out of the way— they were having problems, she had even contacted a divorce attorney—but I don't know about Lily. From what Steve said, with the election coming up, Dean Clark was hoping to pull sympathy votes thanks to his wife's death. He'd already hired a publicist to handle the press and manipulate the public's opinion of him."

"So, he was planning on killing two birds? Using his wife's death to avoid public scrutiny and also to gain votes? He was pandering to the public's sympathies to win?"

"Are you really surprised? What won't a seasoned politician do to make people bend to their whims?"

"You have a point." Elle nodded. "If it turns out that he was planning on having Lily murdered, too, what do you think will happen to the senator?"

"Regardless of what he had intended, we will arrest him for a murder-for-hire plot, but what else the district attorney will go for is up to her—I'm hoping homicide gets added to his charges. The good news is that, no matter how good a lawyer he has, he will be going to prison. And if they prove that he was also planning on killing his daughter, then I'm sure he will likely never leave that prison."

"And what will happen to Lily? Where does she go from here?" She hugged Lily tighter.

He sighed, knowing it was unlikely she was going to like the answer. "She will go into the care of CPS for now while they try to contact the next of kin. If they agree to take her, then they will be her legal acting guardians."

She nibbled on her lip. "I would ask that they go to Catherine's side."

He nodded. "I'll make sure to recommend that to protective services."

"I know that they have a large, distinguished family, so I'm sure they will take her, but I would love it if I could come and see her once in a while."

He reached over and brushed a strand of her brunette hair out of her face and pushed it gently behind her ear. "You saved this little girl's life. She is alive because of your quick actions and unwavering efforts to find her. I'm sure that no one would have a problem with you seeing her. You are her hero."

She smiled and tears welled in her eyes.

"Elle, you're *my* hero." He smiled. "And I hope you know I love you."

She reached over and took his hand in hers.

"You don't have to say that if you don't really mean it. It's okay. You don't owe me that."

"Elle, you know I say what I mean. And I may be slow to know my own feelings, but there is no question in my heart about how I feel about you. I *love* you. I know we haven't been together for all that long, but I can't wait to see where things go. And, as cheesy as this might sound, I can see being with you forever."

"I love you, too, Grant." She smiled, and a tear trembled at the corner of her eye. "And I can see loving you always. You are the man I've been searching for."

He leaned in and gently kissed her lips. "And you are the woman I can't imagine spending a moment without."

There was the sound of clicking, like toenails on tile, and then there was a knock on the door. Grant stood up.

Standing in the doorway looking at them, wiggling manically, was Daisy. She wore an inflatable tube-shaped blue collar, and the effect made him chuckle. The dog didn't seem to notice; she only had eyes for Elle. If anything, he could understand the dog's need to be near her.

"I hope we're not interrupting," Zoey said, smiling. "But someone needed her mom. She's been whining ever since we left the vet's office."

Elle smiled widely. "Oh, Zoey, thank you so much. Is she doing okay?"

Zoey nodded. "She has a few stitches and will have to wear the inflatable collar for a while to make sure she doesn't get at her stitches, but she will be fine."

"What about the other dog?" Grant asked. "If she doesn't have anyone, I have a buddy who has been looking. We can get her a home."

"That would be perfect." Zoey smiled. "And speaking of home, Elle, you are welcome to come back to our team whenever you and Daisy are ready." Zoey let go of the dog's lead.

Daisy was a black dart as she charged past him and jumped into the bed beside Elle. She lay down and started licking Elle's face wildly, nudging Lily awake.

Lily opened her eyes and smiled at Daisy. Just when Grant had thought there was no sweeter sound than hearing Elle say, "I love you," Lily started to giggle. He had never experienced a moment more pure or entirely perfect, and in the sound, he knew he had found his future.

* * * * *

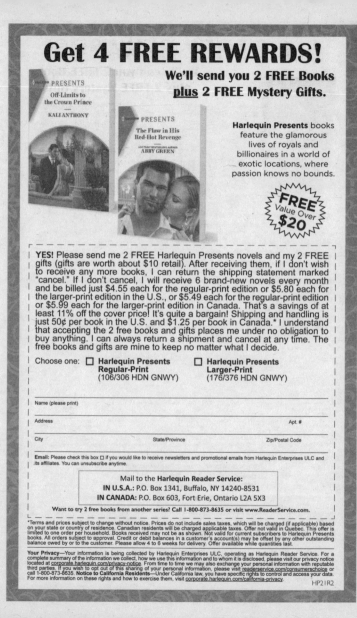

Get 4 FREE REWARDS!

We'll send you 2 FREE Books
plus 2 FREE Mystery Gifts.

Worldwide Library books feature gripping mysteries from "whodunits" to police procedurals and courtroom dramas.

FREE Value Over $20

YES! Please send me 2 FREE novels from the Worldwide Library series and my 2 FREE gifts (gifts are worth about $10 retail). After receiving them, if I don't wish to receive any more books, I can return the shipping statement marked "cancel." If I don't cancel, I will receive 4 brand-new novels every month and be billed just $6.24 per book in the U.S. or $6.74 per book in Canada. That's a savings of at least 22% off the cover price. It's quite a bargain! Shipping and handling is just 50¢ per book in the U.S. and $1.25 per book in Canada.* I understand that accepting the 2 free books and gifts places me under no obligation to buy anything. I can always return a shipment and cancel at any time. The free books and gifts are mine to keep no matter what I decide.

414/424 WDN GNNZ

Name (please print)

Address   Apt. #

City   State/Province   Zip/Postal Code

Email: Please check this box ☐ if you would like to receive newsletters and promotional emails from Harlequin Enterprises ULC and its affiliates. You can unsubscribe anytime.

Mail to the Harlequin Reader Service:
IN U.S.A.: P.O. Box 1341, Buffalo, NY 14240-8531
IN CANADA: P.O. Box 603, Fort Erie, Ontario L2A 5X3

Want to try 2 free books from another series! Call 1-800-873-8635 or visit www.ReaderService.com.

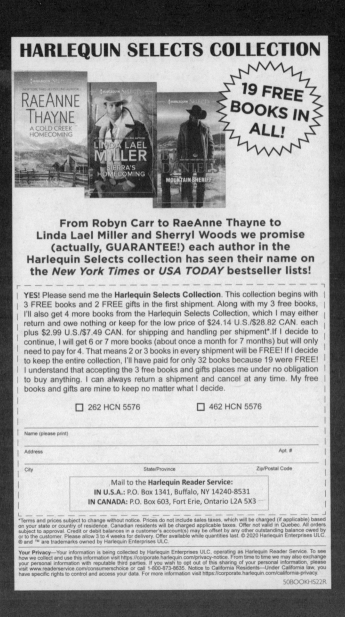